SET-UP WITH THE RANCHER

BARB HAN

Editing: Ali Williams

Cover Design: Jacob's Cover Designs

To my family for unwavering love and support. I can't imagine doing life with anyone else. I love you guys with all my heart.

G rayson Firebrand had drawn the short straw. Doing a favor for a longtime family friend was one thing; leaving the ranch for an unspecified amount of time for a glorified babysitting assignment with a princess was a whole different ballgame. He gripped the steering wheel a little tighter on what had turned out to be a cloudy early September day. The long drive in hundred-plus degree heat and enough humidity to cause him to soak through his shirt during a ten-minute gas stop, was wearing thin. Grayson wasn't sure what was worse, being forced to wear a shirt with buttons or being soaking wet in one.

At least the long, slow drive was behind him. Traffic had been a nightmare. He searched for guest parking as he pulled up to the Turtle Creek Blvd high rise. The thought of all these people living on top of each other in nothing much bigger than a box made him want to loosen his collar more than he already did.

An attendant dressed in a white polo and navy dress shorts waved Grayson over. He drove his dual-cab Chevy pickup under the brightly lit canopy that reminded him of a

Vegas hotel. This tower had thirty-three floors. The princess occupied an apartment on the thirty-second. Princess Kyra Triesen's family was somehow connected to his mother's side. Admittedly, Grayson had been too busy sulking to grab a whole lot of the details of how and why. But an image stamped his thoughts of a tiara-wearing, pampered, and demanding person who couldn't fight her way out of a paper bag.

Dress Shorts reached for the handle as Grayson put the gearshift in park. He beat Blaise, as his nametag read, to opening the door by a fraction of a second.

"Thanks, but I got it." Grayson didn't want to come off as rude, but he couldn't force a smile, and he was fully capable of opening his own door. A courtesy nod would have to suffice.

"Miss K.T. is expecting you," Blaise said as he took a step back and smiled. He was a good height at just shy of six feet tall but looked to be college aged and had yet to fill out his frame. Granted, the young man was a valet, but he didn't look to be able to handle himself in a fight should the need arise. Grayson took note. Depending on how serious this favor became, he might need to provide a replacement.

"That's right," Grayson said. "And I know where I'm headed, so..."

"I'll take care of your vehicle, sir," Blaise said, holding one half of a ticket in his hand as he reached through the opening to place the other piece on top of the dash. In two seconds, Grayson could have just broken the valet's arm by simply slamming the door shut.

He surveyed the area. An entrance to a wooded walking trail sat across the street. Not exactly the nature he was used to. It was, however, the closest thing to nature in this sea of concrete and more tempting than Grayson wanted to admit.

He saw how easy it would be to climb a tree and take aim. A skilled marksman could score a hit from there. The high floor would complicate the shot, but it wouldn't make it impossible.

"I appreciate it, Blaise." Grayson used the man's name out of courtesy as he reached into his front pocket and peeled off a hundred-dollar bill.

"Oh, I'm not..." The attendant shook his head as his gaze darted around on the ground. Grayson recognized the look immediately. It was the same one as Fletcher from third grade when he'd cheated off Grayson's math test. Fletcher denied it when he got caught. Little did Fletcher know, Grayson was dyslexic and had flipped a few of the numbers while working out the problem. Mrs. Marble knew Fletcher had lied when his numbers exactly matched Grayson's.

"My name is Lance." He plucked at the white polo. "I had to borrow a shirt from the laundry and didn't realize a nametag was still on it."

The little hairs on the back of Grayson's neck stood up. "Is that common practice?"

"Yeah, but please don't tell my supervisor. I need this job," Lance pleaded.

"Your secret is safe with me," Grayson stated, firing off a wink as he handed over the money. The gesture and the tip did the trick. Lance's face muscles relaxed, and he nodded. At the very least, Grayson hoped he'd made an ally. The staff's lax security practices were of concern, and he could use all the information he could get. His experience fell on the opposite end of the spectrum; he was used to tracking poachers, not hiding from them while someone else did the hard work.

"Thank you," Lance stated. "I'll take good care of your truck."

"I'd appreciate it if you'd let me know if anyone shows up asking about my friend," Grayson said.

"You got it, sir," Lance said, looking like he appreciated the confidence in him.

Grayson entered the building, crossed the black marble-floored lobby, and headed toward the gold elevator bank. As far as hiding places went, he had no idea how a Dallas high-rise stacked up. All he knew for certain was the princess waited upstairs.

The elevator ride caused his stomach to drop like he was twelve years old again and on the Texas Giant roller coaster. Him and his brothers had been let loose on a local amusement park after bringing stock to the State Fair. He didn't like the sensation then, and he didn't like it now.

Grayson reached for the handrail as the box made of not much more than wires, metal, and glass zipped up to the thirty-second floor. It landed with a *ding* and he got just a little bit of air. A thin sheen of sweat trickled down his forehead. He wiped it away with the back of his sleeve as the doors opened. The magic number he was searching for as he stepped out was three-hundred-twenty-two.

The apartment was directly across the hall. The door was cracked open. There were no lights on inside. A cold chill raced up his spine as he scanned the hallway. Twin security cameras bookended the place. The only sound came from a TV in the apartment next to the elevators.

In one fluid motion, Grayson crossed to the door. He stopped and listened. Lance must have called up to alert the princess. On second thought, wouldn't there be a light on? Would someone in hiding leave the door cracked or would they want to check the peephole before opening the door to anyone? His money was on the latter.

Grayson took a knee, bending down so he could retrieve

his Sig Sauer from an ankle holster. He was used to carrying everywhere we went because he never knew when he might get a call to track poachers. They were a dangerous threat, and he was one of the best trackers in Texas. He figured it was part of the reason for the short straw. The other, most likely bigger part, was that six of his eight brothers had married over the summer in what had to be some kind of record. There were only two single men left other than him. At thirty-one years old, he was the oldest of the three. The straw draw couldn't have been random and he didn't appreciate the set-up.

Right now, though, he had bigger priorities. Like getting inside the apartment undetected.

"Door's open." The female voice was the closest thing to fingernails on a chalkboard he'd heard today. It went straight down his back. Princess? Why had he expected her voice to be different? Pleasing? Wasn't that part of finishing school or whatever small European countries sent their royalty to?

Since this could be a trap, he palmed his weapon and let his index finger hover over the safety mechanism. Slowly, he pushed the heavy oak door until a light flipped on in the kitchen.

"Come on in," K.T. said. The impatience in her voice struck a sour chord. Being careless while in hiding, and short with someone who was there to help, ranked right up there with *too stupid to live* in his opinion. But Grayson had given his word—to his mother no less—and had every intention of following through with his promise to protect the princess.

Grayson stepped inside the apartment, closed and locked the door behind him. He'd been in plenty of situations while hunting poachers but never while surrounded by concrete walls. The hallway was roughly eight feet long. Halfway down and to the right, a door was opened. His best guess was a hall bath. It would be a little too easy for someone to be hiding inside. Only an amateur would walk right on by without clearing the room first.

The wood flooring creaked as he took a step. It was probably by accident but he appreciated the fact anyway. The sound would be enough of a warning for him to prepare.

Back against the wall, he led with his Sig Sauer. A number of scenarios ran through his mind. The princess could be in trouble. Someone could have gotten here first and could be forcing her to invite him in. Otherwise, why wasn't she coming to the door to greet him?

This is where not knowing her or her personality put him at a serious disadvantage. The most recent picture his mother had of the princess showed a too-skinny ten-year-old in braids. Grayson had no memories of the kid visiting the ranch, but he'd been busy with chores and it had seemed like someone was always coming and going while they were growing up. He hadn't paid a whole lot of attention to anyone or anything that didn't directly pertain to him.

A few steps in, the half-bath was visible. No one could fit in there without being obvious.

"What's taking you so long?" the princess asked, the demand rising in her voice. There was something entitled-sounding in her tone. Then again, she was a princess and probably used to getting anything she wanted with the snap of her fingers.

The mouth of the hall opened to an open-concept space. To the left, the kitchen had a rather large white granite island. It was impossible to get a visual read on the entire room due to the massive hunk in the center. On the right, a woman stood at the window as another sat beside her.

"Princess?" he asked, but it was more statement than question.

A small nod indicated she was.

There was an air of elegance surrounding the princess. She wore a silk blouse with similar pants that opened at the cuffs. Her long, straight black-as-pitch hair ran halfway down her back. But it was the woman sitting beside her that caught his gaze and held onto it. There was something about her creamy delicate skin that fisted his heart. Hair that was thicker than a horse's mane and nothing but curls fell down past her shoulders. The most honest, penetrating, bluest eyes blinked at him. She immediately turned her gaze away and back to the princess, who he assumed was her boss.

"I'm Kyra." She crossed the room, meeting him halfway. "Your mother sent a picture of you ahead of time so I would know who you were."

"Grayson, but I guess you already know that," he said.

Kyra stuck her hand out between them as he attempted to look past her to the curly-haired beauty who didn't budge. He shook Kyra's hand.

"Shouldn't that be Princess Kyra?" he asked. "I don't want to break any protocols."

Kyra shook her head and her forehead creased. Up close, she had big honey-brown eyes and soft features.

"I'm not up to speed on all the facts, but I have to ask why you thought it was a good idea to leave the door unlocked," he said.

"The building is secured. The valet called ahead," Kyra blinked at him.

"From what I've been told, there's a serious threat to

your life. This point forward, you trust no one but me," he said. Could she really be that naïve? He reminded himself she was someone who most likely grew up in a guarded tower. And she looked the part draped with a necklace that had to be worth more than a year's salary at the ranch.

"Isn't that why you're here?" she asked, raising a delicate eyebrow.

A thump-sound came from the hallway. Grayson whirled around and put his hand out behind him to indicate the princess should get down. From the corner of his eye, he saw her maid immediately move to cover her.

"It might be nothing," he said, realizing he hadn't had a chance to familiarize himself with the layout of the apartment, let alone the building. He hoped this was a false alarm. Then again, the princess seemed to have been pretty careless up to now. It wouldn't surprise him if she'd left a breadcrumb trail several miles long.

Grayson tightened his grip on his weapon. The lightweight gun was a perfect fit for his ankle holster and just as deadly as a weapon of any size. A bullet was a bullet. With his back against the wall, he moved down the hallway at a fast clip. Halfway there, the door burst open.

"Freeze or I'll shoot," Grayson shouted.

The hallway light was out. A dark figure loomed. The face was darkened but his outline revealed the moment he reached for a gun. A metal star whizzed past Grayson's ear with a whistle. The weapon hit its mark because the dark figure took a step back, giving Grayson the extra second he needed to launch into the bastard.

Grayson dove toward the stranger's knees. A crack sound at the moment of contact said a bone had snapped. The man flew back, his head slamming against the twelve-inch baseboard. The next thing Grayson knew, the maid was beside them with a piece of wire.

"Is he dead?" she asked, bending toward them. Her voice was silk against his skin.

"Don't get too close," he said, checking the man's pulse at the base of his neck. "Great aim, by the way."

"Thank you," she said, not moving an inch while she held out the thin wire.

"He's alive," he reported, taking the offering.

"That means he's knocked out. He won't stay that way for long," she said, moving to his feet. She grabbed his ankles and twisted.

"What are you doing?" he asked.

"Trying to flip him over so you can tie his hands off behind his back," she said in a scolding schoolteacher voice.

He almost cracked a smile.

Grayson eased some of his weight off the creep before helping flip him over. He tied off his hands before they both grabbed a leg, and then dragged him inside the apartment.

"I'll clean up the blood," the maid said. She moved to the kitchen and grabbed supplies as he heard the princess speaking to a 911 dispatcher.

"Don't touch the blood," said Grayson quickly. "The police will need it to corroborate our story of what happened."

The maid shook her head as she moved past him. "We won't be here long enough to tell them personally. I... Princess Kyra...can't be seen here."

"What are you suggesting we call this in as?" he asked, the back of his brain started trying to work something out, but he wasn't exactly certain what that was just yet. It was a feeling like dots that needed connecting but weren't and he couldn't pinpoint the reason.

"An anonymous tip," she said. "They'll find him in here. We'll leave the door ajar."

"Sounds like you've been through this before," he stated as he turned to the princess. She had a panicked look on her face that pinched her eyebrows together.

She shot him a look.

"Fair point." He dragged the body into the living room as the princess stepped aside. He snapped a picture of the intruder's face using the camera on his cell phone.

The woman was clearly shaken, as she should be. She looked to her maid, bowed her head slightly, and said, "The police will be here soon, Princess—"

The puzzle pieces clicked together for Grayson. The 'thing' that he couldn't quite pinpoint connected. The so-called maid had made the mistake of saying, *I* instead of *Princess Kyra* a few moments ago.

Clever trick. This wasn't the time to sort out the details. He was, however, impressed with just how adept the real princess was, and just how willing she'd been to roll up her sleeves and do the dirty work. What other surprises did she have up her sleeves?

2

Kyra grabbed hold of her best friend Zoya as Grayson ushered them toward the elevator bank. She should have known Grayson would be tall and muscled, that was a given, but his sheer and utter good looks caught her off guard. Kyra set those thoughts aside for now, instead focusing on her friend. Zoya probably regretted insisting on coming to America. Kyra would convince her friend to head home or to another country where she could be tucked away safely until Kyra's family diffused the threat.

The bell dinged, indicating the doors were about to open. The sound triggered her fight, flight, or freeze response. Adrenaline pulsed, causing her heart to pound the inside of her ribs. The last time she escaped a safehouse, two guys wearing ski masks and carrying assault rifles had been on the other side, waiting for her.

She held her breath until she could see the elevator was empty. On a sharp sigh, she rushed inside, holding tightly to Zoya's arm. She noted that Grayson Firebrand had put himself in between her and the elevator, and had kept his weapon in his hand. His presence brought a sense of unexpected calmness over her and made her feel safer despite the very real reminder she was running for her life.

Zoya cried softly. Kyra did her best to comfort her friend. Being here was a huge mistake. Surely Zoya saw it now too. Kyra could only pray her father was safe. Her kidnapping would put him at a huge disadvantage. It was common knowledge she was his weak spot. A very bad man was trying to take over her homeland. Criminals were running weapons through Serentia. The people were revolting, demanding protection. This was the perfect time for someone to challenge her father's role as king.

Kyra couldn't allow anyone to use her to manipulate her father.

The elevator hit the lobby floor. Again, Grayson stepped in front of Kyra and her best friend as the doors opened. Thankfully, the lobby was empty. Grayson made a beeline for the attendant.

"Do you want me to bring your truck around, sir?" Lance jumped up from the stool he'd been perched on near the glass double doors.

"No, thank you. All I need are the keys," Grayson said.

Lance immediately retrieved them and tossed them over. Grayson caught them like a professional baseball player. She'd seen the sport on TV in her father's private chamber.

With a nod, the tall and drop-dead gorgeous man with the purest blue eyes led them to his vehicle that was parked near the doors. There was something about his masculine presence that sent sensual shivers skittering across her skin. He opened the passenger side first. She hustled inside, pulling Zoya next to her.

"Stay low," Kyra said to Zoya. Her friend's eyes were still

wide and her skin was bleached-sheet white. Was she in shock?

Kyra couldn't let herself think about what a close call that had been as she climbed into the passenger seat and scooted away from the door. She took in a few deep, measured breaths. They only served to invite the spicy, masculine scent of the driver who sat so close beside her their outer thighs touched. Grayson Firebrand had it all; height, body for days, and looks that could literally stop traffic. She guessed him to be close to six-feet-four-inches with a trim but muscled body. This wasn't the time to think about how his torso formed an improbable V. Or about those thick lashes that framed irises so clear blue they made her long for the sea back home. He had just enough scruff on his chin to make her wonder what it would feel like against her skin.

Suddenly, Kyra's mouth dried up. She swallowed to ease the dryness and refocused her attention on her best friend.

"It'll be okay," she soothed as Grayson navigated them through one-way street after one-way street until they ended up on a highway and then on a toll road heading south.

Zoya softly cried against Kyra's shoulder. They stayed that way until Grayson pulled up in front of an all-suite hotel a block from the highway in a residential community in a city by the name of Frisco.

"Where are we?" she asked.

"At a safe place to spend the night," he said.

"How do you know?" she asked, annoyed by his brusqueness despite being relieved that he must have a plan.

"Because my parents are friends with the owners of this hotel chain." He parked before retrieving his cell phone from his pocket. He sent off a text. The response came back almost immediately. "All we have to do is hold tight for a few minutes while my mom works in the background."

"Doing what?" she asked as his timbre traveled over her and through her, causing her stomach to free fall and her body to warm.

"Making arrangements for us to stay here without having to sign any paperwork or give away our identities. It'll be like we were never here in the first place," he said. "But first, we wait until I get the okay."

"I'm impressed," she said, not bothering to hide her shock.

"How so, Princess?" he asked, and she picked up on the surprise in his tone.

"For starters, you can stop calling me that," she countered, uncomfortable with everything associated with that title.

"I didn't mean to offend you." There was a genuine note in his tone that made her reassess her response to his words.

"I'm not usually so easy to insult," she admitted.

"Will your maid be okay?" he asked in a low whisper as Zoya cried softly.

"Who? Zoya?" She really was caught off guard now. And then it dawned on her what he must be thinking. "She's my best friend. We're practically like sisters."

"How is she doing over there?" he whispered.

"Not great," Kyra admitted quietly. She'd never seen her best friend this shell-shocked before. "I warned her not to come with me. She insisted. We might have grown up like sisters but she isn't used to this side of my life. She's been away working on a PhD for ages."

"Hey, Zoya," he said in a normal voice. "What interests

you so much that you would be willing to sign up for the torture of a PhD?"

Zoya perked up just a little bit. Kyra took it as a good sign.

"Archeology," she said, and her voice was so small that it nearly broke Kyra's heart.

"What made you want to devote this much of your life to studying bones?" he asked.

"It's so much more than that." Zoya perked up a bit more, sniffling and rubbing the tears from her eyes. "It's history with proof."

"I guess I've never heard it put quite like that before," he stated as a text came in. "Room seven."

"My lucky number," Kyra whispered.

Zoya must have taken this news as a good sign because she sat a little straighter. She'd always been superstitious.

Grayson insisted on coming around to the passenger side of the truck to open the door for them. He mumbled something about doing it so he could get the lay of the land, and check for any threat. He also said people here expected it and not to do so would make them stick out if anyone was watching or happened to drive past.

There was a couple dozen vehicles of various types parked in the lot. An RV ran the entire length of the back wall. Kyra took it all in, checking for quick exits as she followed Grayson toward the lobby.

"When we get close to the front door, feel free to duck your heads together to make it difficult for the cameras to pick up the details of your faces," he said. It was then she saw that he was holding something in his hand. He placed the object on his head, and she realized it was a baseball cap. He tugged the front down and tucked his chin to his chest in a definite move to block camera footage.

Kyra didn't look up again until they were inside room seven. An attendant had cracked the door open and then left a pair of keys inside. Despite being away from each other over the past seven years since Zoya left to go to university, Kyra still knew her best friend. They had the kind of lifelong connection that picked right back up where it left off no matter how much time passed in between visits.

The second the place was secure, Zoya exhaled a breath so big her shoulders literally deflated. They were safe for now. But how long would it last?

GRAYSON MOVED to the coffee maker and started a cup.

"Anyone else want one?" he asked.

"Yes, but I can make it myself," Kyra said. A princess who didn't need to be pampered. He couldn't have been more off the mark with his initial assessment of her. She had mad skills with a metal star too. He reminded himself to ask her about it later when her friend was out of earshot. Zoya didn't seem in the right state of mind for a lengthy discussion about what had just happened.

"No worries," he said. "I'm already here."

The first cup was ready in less than two minutes.

"How do you take yours?" He figured there were packets of sugar and creamer around here somewhere.

"Black," she stated, plain as day.

He handed over a cup and ignored the frisson of heat at the point of contact where their fingers grazed, chalking it up to his body being on high alert. A near-death experience heightened senses as part of the adrenaline rush. Basic biology meant he needed proof of life, which normally came in the form of procreating. Since he was an adult and not a wild animal, he knew to push those instincts aside. Instincts that had him wanting to haul Kyra against his chest and claim those heart-shaped lips.

Besides, one look at her friend's suffering was a water bucket on a campfire when it came to putting out sexual desire.

"I'm clearly late to the game here," he said after taking a sip of fresh brew. The coffee was weak but he wasn't about to complain.

"Is there tea?" Zoya asked as Kyra sat beside her friend and placed a comforting arm around her shoulders.

"Let's see here." He checked the box. "English breakfast or chamomile?"

"Chamomile, if you don't mind," Zoya said. Her unfocused gaze gave him the impression she was still in shock. At least she was talking.

He fixed her tea and handed over the cup.

"Thank you," Zoya said as Kyra mouthed the same words. It was easy to see the close bond between the friends even though he'd been surprised to discover they were friends and not princess and servant. The realization had him questioning all his previous assumptions about Kyra.

"Tell me, how do you know my parents?" Grayson asked.

"I don't," Kyra said. "My mom came to America to study and she and your mother somehow met."

"You never asked your mother about it?" He'd figured girls and mothers were close, but then his mother had nine boys. She loved them dearly but never made a secret out of wishing she'd had at least one girl.

"She died when I was a girl." Kyra gave a slight headshake. A sadness brewed behind those incredible eyes of hers at the mention of her mother. His heart went out to her.

"I'm sorry," he said with all the compassion he could muster.

"My father raised me," she said. "Which probably explains why I was trained in martial arts, instead of going to finishing school. I'm certain my mother would be shocked if she saw me now."

"Or proud," he said. "I'd fight beside you any day of the week."

Her eyes lit up for the briefest moment and it had the effect of him taking a sucker punch in the center of his chest. His reaction to the princess caught him off guard as much as his attraction did. She had the most penetrating set of honest blue eyes that had a way of seeming like they were looking right through him. He reminded himself of the job he was here to do. Keeping her alive and safe might prove more difficult than he'd initially believed possible.

"It doesn't really work like that in our culture," Kyra said.

"I'm not so sure," Zoya interceded. "My parents allowed me to get an overseas education rather than stay home and find a husband."

"True," Kyra agreed. She didn't point out that she was a monarch. The rules were different for her.

"My mother knew yours and I believe she would be proud," Zoya said.

"I'm sure you're right," Kyra stated with about as much enthusiasm as a mom reading the nutrition label on a cereal box.

Zoya seemed completely unaware of the change in Kyra's expression. She'd gone from a serious expression to a consoling smile. The move was most likely meant to reassure her friend. Hearing from others who knew her mother more than she ever would didn't seem to bring the intended comfort. In fact, it downright made her sad. Grayson had to fight the urge to reach out to her, to be her comfort.

"Have you ever seen this man before in your life?" Grayson moved the conversation back on track, producing the cell phone picture.

Kyra examined it before shaking her head. "It's possible he's a paid assassin," she admitted. "Although, it's likely the people who are after me want to use me as leverage against my father. It doesn't hurt that they'd also be removing his sole heir."

"Complicated situation," he stated.

Kyra nodded before taking a sip of coffee. The corners of her mouth turned down ever so slightly as she moved the cup away from her lips. Her nose wrinkled just enough to give her reaction away and he couldn't agree more. The coffee tasted more like flavored water than fresh brew. But it was all they had at the moment and would have to do.

"Hold on a minute," Zoya said. "Doesn't he look a little bit like Pietro's brother?"

Kyra studied the picture.

"It would be impossible." Kyra shook her head. "There's no way."

"You can't deny the resemblance," she said.

Kyra took in a deep breath and then pinched the bridge of her nose. "I won't deny that he looks like Pietro's brother. But his brother is in prison. And even if he wasn't, he would never set foot in America."

"What if he was bringing a message to you?" Zoya said.

"There was only one message he brought, and it involved a gun," Grayson stated.

Zoya nodded.

Kyra looked up at him with heavy eyes. "What's next?" she asked.

"I'm used to tracking folks, not hiding from them, so I need to make a few mental adjustments as we go. How will you know when it's safe to go home again?" he asked. His heart took a hit when their eyes locked. It was as though an unseen force hit him with enough power to knock him back a few steps. Something that felt a whole lot like desire welled up as an ache formed in his chest. What was he supposed to do with that?

3

"My father will get a message to me." Kyra had been stripped of her home, her family, and now all she had left was literally the clothes on her back. Hiding, when all she really wanted to do was fight back, made her long to kick something. Preferably a punching bag like she did when she was back home. Kick-boxing was more than a great workout. It was a way to destress.

Right now, though, her priority was Zoya.

Grayson nodded. There was something about the way he moved when he walked across the room to bring a chair over that released a dozen butterflies in her stomach. There was a beauty to his strength, and athleticism. He walked in long, decisive steps like a fine-tuned athlete.

She purposely turned her attention toward her best friend. "No one knows you're with me and no one wants to harm you. You are innocent in all this and I don't know if I can protect you. I don't even know if I can protect myself."

Glancing up to see that Grayson was studying her as she spoke wasn't the best move. Her heart fluttered like a schoolgirl's when she saw her crush. Except this man stirred a physical reaction from her body that was far more mature, more primal than anything she'd experienced before. The moth-to-flame draw to him was mesmerizing. Kyra cleared her throat and refocused.

Head down, Zoya kept quiet, which meant she was in deep thought. Kyra took it as a good sign that her friend was listening, considering. She decided to keep going.

"Besides, it'll be easier for Grayson if it's just the two of us. Right, Grayson?" Kyra brought her gaze up to meet his again and shot a quick look. She hoped he picked up on the plea for help.

His quick nod said he did and some of the pressure sitting heavy on her shoulders lifted.

"Kyra is right. The fewer people, the better from my perspective. It'll make it easier to move freely and I have a feeling we'll be doing just that until this situation is resolved," he explained. "You're welcome to stay with us, Zoya. I'm not telling you what to do here. Just suggesting it'll be easier to move if we sell ourselves as a couple."

A sensual tremor vibrated through Kyra at Grayson's last word, a tremor she needed to rein in. The only thing worse than having it was the thought he might realize the effect he had on her.

Zoya's gaze came up swiftly. "I don't want to be in the way," she said. "Or make this any harder for Kyra than it already is."

Oh, she'd jumped at that idea pretty quickly. Had she been looking for an out? If so, Kyra was relieved she gave her friend one. This was already a lot for Kyra to deal with, and she really didn't want to drag her best friend into danger too.

"You'd be doing us a favor," Kyra reassured.

"Are you sure?" Zoya's momentary hesitation was replaced by hopeful eyes.

"One hundred percent," Kyra stated. She put her arm around Zoya's shoulders. "You'd be doing us a huge favor."

"Only if it's good for you," Zoya stated, but the relief in her voice said she desperately needed to go.

"It is," Kyra said again. "I need you safe for when this whole ordeal is behind us, and I can come back home."

Zoya nodded.

"I can make arrangements," Grayson said. "Just let me know a final destination so I can figure out the best route to get there."

"Probably Canada," Zoya said. "Vancouver. I have friends there who share an apartment."

True to his word, Grayson immediately started working on his cell phone. Zoya's mood brightened and some of the tension lines on her forehead eased. Her deep-set eyes still held concern for Kyra. There was no denying it.

"Stay safe," Zoya said, reaching over for a hug.

Kyra held her friend until Grayson said a car was waiting out front. He put his baseball cap on Zoya before walking her outside alone. When he returned, he held two bags in his hands. The first was the size and shape of a full garbage bag. The second was a much smaller white bag with orange stripes that made a W. The smell of hamburgers filled the room and her stomach growled, causing her to realize just how hungry she was and how long it had been since she'd eaten anything.

"Whataburger," Grayson said, holding up the striped bag.

She stood up and met him at the work desk, arranging the pull-out table in between the edge of the bed and the office chair. She motioned for him to take the chair before perching herself on the edge of the bed.

He set out two burgers in wrappers and a mountain of fries in between them on a napkin he'd spread out. "I hope you like cheese."

"Is that a serious question?" she quipped, grateful for the lighter conversation. The day had been hard. The evening downright scary. That was the closest she'd come to being killed since she'd been on the run over the past few days and the reality of her situation descended around her shoulders like a heavy blanket weighting her limbs. "In case I wasn't clear. I love every kind of cheese."

His smile could warm the coldest night. A fluttering sensation released in her stomach. Her heart beat faster in her chest and her hands got cold and clammy. Suddenly, she was hyper-aware of him sitting so close to her. A similar feeling had struck inside the truck. She decided to chalk every bit of it up to the fact she'd almost died and her nerves were most likely completely out of whack. It definitely wasn't a real attraction. It couldn't be a real attraction.

Kyra opened the wrapper and wasted no time taking a bite. She mewled with pleasure as she chewed on the juicy bit of perfection. The crispiness of the white onion and lettuce, the sour crunch of the pickle along with the mix of condiments were everything a fast-food burger should be. Before she knew it, the wrapper was empty, and probably more than her fair share of fries were gone. She polished off the Coke next before glancing over and seeing that Grayson was still eating.

"Sorry, I was hungrier than I realized," she said.

"Never apologize for eating," he said before quirking a smile. He seemed pleased that she'd enjoyed her food.

"I've always heard about American fast food," she said,

wiping the corners of her mouth with a napkin. "Now, I understand how great it is."

"Not all places are this good. Believe me," he said, tension relaxing in his eyes as he sat back in the chair. He handed over a bottle of water. "Drink plenty of this. In the meantime, tell me everything that happened to bring you to the condo."

"I'd been careful, so I left my personal cell phone in a café bathroom in Kelariz so no one would suspect I was missing. I had a backup phone that only a few people in my inner circle were aware of. It probably sounds like a lot to an outsider but I had to be careful. The people after me will do anything and everything to torture my father if they catch me. It's well known that my father loves me. We've been close since it was just the two us after my mother died. He would do anything to for me and these guys must know it," she explained. "Next, I hid in the trunk of a black SUV, then jumped into a Jeep Wrangler as my getaway crew raced from my small village to the sea. A dinghy waited there on the beach and once we got far enough away from shore, we switched to wave runners."

"And then?" he asked, leaning forward and resting his elbows on his knees.

"One of my crew arranged for a sheikh's yacht to be waiting for us there, idling," she continued. "We headed toward Canada so I could cross the border at Toronto. But then there was a threat we hadn't anticipated. One of my crew found a spyware tool that had hacked into my backup phone. It's a tracking tool. He noticed it almost a week into the escape and too late to stop. There was an encounter with a speed boat that ended in loss of life. My phone went into the sea and my crew had to split up. I picked up Zoya in Canada where she practically forced me to let her come to

America with me. The crew was supposed to meet up at the condo in two days' time."

"I'm guessing your father somehow got ahold of my mother in the meantime to send me up to help," he assessed.

"I'm sorry for putting your life in danger," she said on a sharp sigh.

"Don't be," he said. "I track poachers on the ranch and it's just as dangerous. Believe me, some of them have nothing to lose and that's not the kind of person you want getting the best of you. I came here of my own free will and I want to help."

Those words, those reassurances, settled her nerves—nerves that were still raw from recent events as her brain tried to play catchup. "The notice to flee my country or be kidnapped and used against my father as leverage to force him to hand over control of our small country had been a matter of minutes.

"From the bottom of my heart, thank you for being here," she said, meaning every word.

"You don't have to thank me. Wouldn't be any other place." Grayson needed to understand as much of the situation they faced as possible. Assessing risk came with the territory. "But tell me who is after your family and why."

"There's a gang called, OMG. They're a motorcycle gang from Finland headed by Tuomo Korhonen. Or at least that's what everyone believes," she stated. "They have links to an organized crime network that is supposedly providing the backup they need."

"A Finnish person could blend right in here in America

with the blond hair," he surmised.

She nodded.

"Another motorcycle club that used to be known as Bandidos from France might be responsible. One of the leaders recently broke off and formed his own club. His name is Claude Emile. Then there's the brother of my security detail, who we recently found out has possible links to organized crime. But Marko Korpi checks out one hundred percent. His brother Veeti is in question," she stated.

"What about your current security detail? Who are the players there?" he asked.

"Joakim Nordegren works directly for me but we call him Pietro," she stated. "And then there's Charlie Joakim but he's my cousin on my mom's side. There's no way he's involved. He's six years older than me and has taken on the role of big brother and protector since the day I was born."

"Where is your security now?" he asked.

"Great question," she stated. "Without my cell phone, no one can reach me. I was given the condo address in Dallas to find once I made it to America. We were headed there anyway and it was supposed to be our rally point if we were somehow busted up."

"How many people knew about the address?" he asked, figuring they might be able to narrow down the suspect list, which included two possible organized crime syndicates, and the brother of her current security detail Veeti.

"No one but Pietro, Charlie, and me," she stated. "Zoya had no idea what was going on when I showed up at her apartment in Canada. She insisted on getting me to my checkpoint and I never should have allowed her to pretend to be me. She saw it in some movie and..."

"I know it's probably hard not to blame yourself for someone else's choices, especially when said choices put them in physical danger. But Zoya is a grown woman. She came into this with the full awareness things could go wrong," he defended.

"She did this out of her love for me and our friendship," she quickly countered, and he could see this point weighed heavily on her mind.

"And she is fine. She's on her way back to Vancouver as we speak. And my instincts say she is proud of herself right now for being able to see a friend through a very rough patch," he stated, hoping she could really hear what he had to say. Blaming herself wasn't productive and a growing part of him wanted her to give herself a break. Kyra came across as the type who would take her friend's safety to heart at a level far beyond most people's ability to care.

Kyra nodded.

A way to pick up her spirits dawned on him. He reached for the garbage bag before tossing it at her feet.

"What's in there?" she asked.

"Take a look," he said, but his comment was met with a look that said she wasn't in the mood for any additional surprises today.

Fair enough.

"There's fresh clothing, pajamas, and toiletries. I made a guess about your sizes," he said before reaching into his front pocket and producing two gold bands. He slid one on his wedding hand before holding the other on the flat of his palm. "Whoever is after you is looking for a single European princess, not a married American."

Her gaze widened in what looked like shock as she took the offering before sliding the gold band on her ring finger. He noticed there were no tan lines and hoped, for reasons he couldn't explain, that meant she wasn't married. Surely, if she was, her husband would be here protecting her, defending her, and stepping in the line of fire for her. A woman like Kyra deserved nothing less.

"I'm not, by the way," she said before adding, "married, that is."

"Neither am I," he added for more reasons he couldn't explain. It suddenly seemed important to him for her to know he wouldn't be letting anyone down at home by putting himself at risk. That if, by chance, he didn't return to the ranch that no one would lose their soulmate. When he really thought about it, it was most likely the reason he'd drawn the short straw on this assignment. Six of his eight brothers had found the loves of their lives over the past few months. It was impossible not to feel like he'd missed the boat somehow, which was ridiculous. Grayson didn't want any additional complications in his life right now. He was still trying to get his mind wrapped around all the changes going on at the ranch since the Marshall's sudden death. Then, there were the recent crimes against and involving his family.

Nothing was the best thing that could happen to him and everyone else on the ranch. They could use a few minutes of quiet to process what had happened and begin to repair relationships with his uncle and cousins.

"Mind if I ask you a couple of questions before I take a shower and change?" she asked, slipping her feet underneath her sweet round bottom—a bottom he had no business staring at no matter how tempting it was.

"I'm an open book," he said, wadding up the empty wrappers before tossing them inside the Whataburger bag. He set the bag outside the door, figuring the smell would drive them crazy all night if he didn't deal with it. While he was there, he put the Do Not Disturb sign on the knob.

"Are you an only child?" she asked before biting back a

yawn. It was a good sign that she seemed to be relaxing around him enough to let herself become tired. It also probably meant that her adrenaline had worn thin. Now that she had a full belly, she would rest better.

He laughed out loud at the question.

"Hardly. I come from a family of nine boys and have nine male cousins who also live on the same ranch," he said.

"That sounds like a whole lot of testosterone in one place," she said on a laugh after the shock seemed to wear off.

"Believe me, it can be," he stated, not even able to go there about all the stress his family had been through in recent months, or the fact his Aunt Jackie had been trying to manipulate his grandfather's will. He was still trying to process the lengths she'd gone to in order to protect her secret and the fact she would spend the rest of her life behind bars as a result.

"I've been an only child my entire life," she said. "I always wished for a sibling."

"They can be a handful and there are a whole mess of strong personalities at the ranch, but I wouldn't trade a big family for the world," he admitted.

"You must wish for one of your own," she stated as a little blush crawled up her neck and to her cheeks, contrasting against creamy skin.

"No kids for me," he said quickly. He'd never given them much thought except to say he couldn't imagine a day when he'd be ready for that level of responsibility. "No rugrats in my future. I have a niece by the name of Angel. Her name fits her too. I've never seen my brother happier despite the lack of sleep. But kiddos of my own are not for me."

The image of Kyra holding a baby of her own suddenly had him re-think his lifelong plan of staying a bachelor.

4

———

Kyra frowned. She couldn't explain the disappointment she felt deep in her chest about Grayson not wanting to become a father. She barely knew the man, despite her heart feeling a connection like she'd never experienced before. Reality said a near-death experience would have heightened her emotions and was possibly blowing everything out of proportion. But, something told her this man was special anyway.

Besides, staying alive was far more important than renumerating about a man, no matter how much like perfection he seemed to be. When she snapped out of her mental fog, he was studying her with a questioning look on his face.

"Everything okay?" he asked. Then, seemed to catch himself. "Never mind. Foolish question. How about taking a shower and getting some rest?"

"Both of those sound amazing," she said with a groan at the thought of standing up again. Adrenaline had faded. Her stomach was full. And there was no word to describe how tired she felt. Going to bed dirty and without brushing her teeth held no appeal.

"These should hopefully fit," he said, holding up a bag.

"Thank you. I'm sure whatever is in there is better than what I'm wearing," she admitted glancing down at the pants and shirt she had on.

"You'd look beautiful in a sack," he said so naturally and so off-handedly that she actually believed him.

"Can I ask a question?" he asked as she managed to get to her feet.

She nodded.

"Where did you learn to throw a star like that?" he asked. The fact he was so impressed filled her with pride.

"My cousin...the one I mentioned earlier...is six years old than I am. Since I never had siblings, the two of us became close. I guess he's always watched out for me and I wanted to do everything he could. Ride a bicycle. Learn martial arts..." she said.

"Doesn't sound like something a princess would be allowed to do," he said.

"My father never wanted to leave me defenseless," she admitted. "I think he saw me hurting after my mother died, so he built up my strength in every other way. I believe he also knew the day might come when I would be alone in the world without him. So, when I asked if I could train with my cousin, my father gave an enthusiastic answer. In fact, his response gave me the impression he'd been thinking about sending me with my cousin long before I asked."

"He sounds like a good person. And forward-thinking," Grayson said as his eyebrow shot up. "I'm impressed."

"Can I ask *you* a question?" She turned the tables on him.

He nodded.

"What impression did you have when you heard I was a princess?" Her curiosity got the best of her and she wanted to know what she was up against. Anytime she traveled overseas she'd been met with all kinds of assumptions about what her life was like. Everything from Princess Jasmine to Snow White and everything in between.

"Probably all the wrong things came to mind," he said. "All the stupid old cliches."

"And what do you think now?" she asked.

"That I need to get my head out of old fairy tales," he said with a grin. "At this point, I'm thinking along the lines of Mulan meets Wonder Woman but in a surprisingly delicate-looking shell."

"You say the word delicate like it's a bad thing." She probably should have accepted her gains right there, except she couldn't without asking. "Is it?"

"Not at all. It adds to your beauty and makes you so much more unexpected," he said, and when they made eye contact, all kinds of warm campfires lit inside her. Was he having the same reaction? Because the one area of her life where she had been sheltered was being around the opposite sex. Unless she'd been blood-related, she had surprisingly little contact with men. At age twenty-five, she was no longer a virgin and yet, despite the men she'd dated so far, she'd always been left feeling like there was so much more out there. No offense to her past, but her relationships had been quite boring. Appropriate, but boring.

"Thank you," she mumbled as she took the bag and then exited to the bathroom like her feet had been set on fire. Other parts of her body had warmed. More things she didn't want to focus on or think about while her nerves were already frazzled. She'd learned to halt a long time ago, meaning she needed to stop momentum on her thoughts when she was hungry, angry, lonely, or tired. She definitely qualified as tired at the moment.

The shower was brief and heavenly. The toothbrush and toothpaste made her mouth happy. And the pajamas fit a little loose around her tiny waist, but they were otherwise spot on. She'd always had the tiny waist, thicker thighs problem. Of course, Zoya had been quick to point out that a tiny waist didn't exactly qualify as a problem. Kyra smiled. The thought her best friend was safe and on her way back to Vancouver made the smile genuine. Showing up on her doorstep a couple of days ago hadn't been meant to turn into the nightmare at the condo.

"Your turn," Kyra said as she joined Grayson.

"I have a duffel in my truck with my supplies," he stated. "Didn't want to leave while you were in the shower."

"Okay," she said. "Any chance you have a spare gun?"

He retrieved a small weapon and handed it over.

"I'm guessing you already know how to use it," he said.

"Most of my training is hand-to-hand combat," she admitted. "My father said the only way to outrun a bullet is to put as much mass in between it and me as possible."

He stood so close to her, causing her body to hum with need as he handed it over. "Smart man."

"Thank you. I'd ask you where you learned to shoot but I'm guessing growing up on a ranch made carrying a weapon necessary," she surmised.

He chuckled and it was a low rumble in his chest. His deep timbre traveled over her and through her.

"You could say we were practically born knowing how to shoot but we were probably more like six or seven when we got our first BB guns," he said. He seemed to realize she had no idea what that was. "It's just a type of air gun that shoots these little BB pellets instead of bullets. We used them to pick cans off the fence or a tree stump. We honed our shooting skills with them. Between those and homemade slingshots we had a field day with Coke bottles and empty cans."

"Sounds like a great childhood with lots of freedom," she said, unable to hide the melancholy in her voice at the contrast with her own.

"Probably sounds better than it was in that respect. Ranching is a seven-day-a-week job. Actually, it's more like a way of life. Endless days with nothing but hard work in front of you. Work after school and sports," he admitted. "Don't get me wrong, ranching is in my blood and Texas is my home. But it's not an easy life for most folks. The day-to-day can be hard and some folks see it as monotonous work."

"You don't," she said. She could see it in his eyes. They lit up as he talked about his home.

"There wasn't a time I didn't know I wanted to be a rancher—despite some teen years that made me rebel against everything familiar," he said.

"Sounds about right," she said. I don't think anyone gets past their teen years without pushing back a little. Besides, it's good to know what you're passionate about."

"What about you, Princess? What do you love?" he asked. His question struck a chord deep inside her in a place she kept hidden, protected.

Her throat dried up and those clammy hands returned. Rather than answer his question, she cleared her throat and took the weapon. The cold metal against her palm was a good distraction.

"The safety is here." His thumb brushed over hers as he brought it to the mechanism.

"Once that's off, I point and shoot...correct?" The question was meant to be rhetorical and draw attention away from the way her arms goose bumped with his slightest touch.

GRAYSON PULLED his hand back and touched the tip of his index finger to his thumb, trying to figure out what was up with the electricity every time he and Kyra touched. His thumb barely grazed her hand and he would have thought there'd been a gas explosion for the effect skin-to-skin contact had on him.

"That's right. Keep the safety on and never point the end of the barrel at someone you don't want to shoot, especially me," he said with a wink, doing his best to ignore his body's reaction.

The glittery look in those honest blue eyes had him rethinking standing this close. A shower would be all the distraction he needed. Plus, then he could concentrate on something besides the way her clean scent reminded him of a perfect sunrise at his favorite time of year.

"Okay then," she said, breaking eye contact. He'd seen that look before and decided this wasn't the time or place to think about starting something up with someone. Besides, he knew on instinct she was special and he had no room in his life for someone like her.

Grayson couldn't have been more wrong about the princess. He was simply caught off guard and that was that.

"I'll be back in a few minutes," he said before grabbing the door key and heading out. There wasn't a whole lot of activity in the all-suite hotel at this time of night. Most seemed bedded down for the evening.

As he walked, he kept his steps light and his head down in case there was a hallway camera, all the way his gaze kept scanning the area. So far, so good. He wasn't expecting trouble because he'd used a few evasive tactics on the way here, not to mention the fact he'd kept watch for signs someone had followed them.

Kyra had no cell phone so he wasn't concerned someone had put a trace on her. The busted meetup at the condo had him the most concerned. Two people knew about the spot aside from Kyra and Zoya, and Zoya seemed like a dedicated friend. Her fear couldn't have been faked; no one was that good an actress. She'd genuinely gone into shock after the encounter. If she'd been part of the setup, something in her body language or reaction would have given her away.

No, Zoya was clean. The only possibility that existed there was that she might have mentioned the location to someone, a friend or relative. But then that didn't make sense either. Unless she knew where they were headed. He needed to ask Kyra if her friend had any prior knowledge of the meetup location in Turtle Creek.

There'd been no visible cell phone on Zoya...hold on. Wait. She'd made the call to 911. If Kyra didn't have a cell then it had to belong to Zoya. He knew of a somewhat shady large company that sold software that could allow someone to install spyware on a cell phone remotely. All the perp had to have was a cell phone number and he could trace her phone. Had Zoya brought it with her to this hotel?

They'd been there a few hours at this point.

Grayson searched the parking lot for anything out of the ordinary. There were only half a dozen vehicles parked. Everything looked copasetic. He grabbed his duffel from his truck before heading back inside.

At the door, he realized he probably should have come up with a signal, a knock, to let her know it was him. She'd been level-headed in the condo fight, so he had to trust she wasn't going to shoot him the second he walked through the door.

Quickly, he tapped the keycard against the door card reader. After turning the handle and opening the door, he immediately whispered, "It's Grayson."

Thankfully, he stepped inside to a gun pointed at the floor and not him.

Kyra moved to the nightstand and set the weapon down with the barrel facing the wall.

"Question," he began. "Did Zoya bring her cell phone with her to the hotel by chance?"

Kyra's gaze unfocused as she looked up and to the left, a sure sign of digging into her brain to retrieve information.

"The last time I remember seeing her with it was the condo," she said. "To be honest, I don't remember her having it on her when we came here. We left in a hurry without grabbing any of our belongings."

"The cops no doubt have the suspect in custody," he said. "I need to think about how to handle the situation back in Turtle Creek."

"My family will take care of it with the police." She flashed eyes at him. "We have diplomatic immunity. I need to get word to my father's contact so the mess can be cleaned up. This is normally something my security detail would handle but I have no idea where they are."

"And vice versa," he pointed out.

"At this point, there doesn't seem to be another option," she stated, biting back a yawn. "As far as Zoya goes, should we call and see if she picks up?"

"I'd rather not have my personal cell phone associated with her in any way," he stated. "If someone has installed spyware in her phone, all her contacts and incoming or outgoing calls are suspect from this point forward. I did, however, ask the security company that I hired to contact me when she was safely on a plane to Vancouver. She will be accompanied to her apartment and I'll provide round the clock security until we know it's safe."

"Are you sure you're just a rancher?" she asked with a quirked brow.

It dawned on him she must not know the Firebrand name. Where should he even begin?

"In Texas, my family are probably considered to be *the* ranchers," he said.

"When you told me about all your brothers and cousins, I couldn't help but think of all those mouths to feed," she said. "You must be pretty successful to be able to arrange the kind of security that could transport Zoya and then keep twenty-four-hour watch. Please excuse my bluntness but I didn't think ranchers would have those kinds of resources."

"Normally, you'd be right. Plenty of ranchers barely get by these days. Think of my family as more of a cattle ranching dynasty," he said. Her eyes widened and she seemed to catch the gist of what he said.

"I must say that I'm impressed," she said. "But not because of your finances. I'm blown away by how down-to-earth you seem. What's the expression?" She hesitated for a long moment as she snapped her fingers. "Wait. Don't tell me." More snapping followed by a smile. "I got it. Salt of the earth type."

Grayson chuckled as she crumbled onto the bed. She slid inside the covers and bit back another yawn.

"A hard day's work will do that to you," he said. The time for getting to know each other on a personal level would come. Right now, she needed rest and he needed to do a little research on the motorcycle gangs she'd mentioned. See if he could find answers.

5

Kyra blinked her eyes open. The room was dimly lit. Grayson sat in the office chair, leaning forward, studying a tablet. Even blurry, he was gorgeous.

"What time is it?" she asked, rubbing her eyes

"Nine o'clock in the morning," he said as he rolled his shoulders like he was trying to work out some of the tension.

"How did I sleep so long?" Panic caused her to sit straight up.

"How much sleep have you gotten in the last week?"

"Apparently, not nearly enough." She pushed up to sitting and fluffed a pillow before placing it behind her back. "What have you been studying?"

"The motorcycle gangs you mentioned." He set the tablet on the desk beside him. "I wanted to learn the faces of the leaders."

"They won't come for me personally." She knew they would send one of the grunts.

"Probably not but I still wanted to learn the players," he

admitted. "By the way, Zoya is on a plane as we speak." He checked the time. "In fact, she'll be landing any minute now."

"Were you able to find out about the cell phone?" she asked.

"My security detail asked her and she didn't have it on her." He compressed his lips into a frown. "But they could still trace her to Dallas where she left it and that's not good."

"True." She excused herself before heading to the bathroom to get rid of her morning breath. When she returned, there was a cup of coffee waiting for her and a power bar. "Thank you for looking after me like this."

"That should be enough protein to buy us a little time to make our next move. We can stop off and get a proper meal when we head out," he said.

"Too bad we can't stay here a while longer. Bed's pretty comfortable," she said, taking a sip of coffee before practically inhaling the bar. It wasn't the best thing she'd ever tasted but wasn't the worst either. At this point, she was grateful to have *anything* in her stomach.

"How would you describe the flavor of the bar?" His eyebrow came up and she noticed he had a small mole just to the left of where it arched.

"Tree bark dipped in mud," she said, thinking how a tiny thing like a mole could make Grayson that much more attractive. His face was perfection and those little flaws made it even more interesting.

"My thoughts exactly." Grayson's laugh—a low rumble —was something she could listen to all day. "It has the most protein, though. Sorry about the taste."

"It got the job done. My stomach stopped growling," she said with a shrug realizing she might have just made him feel bad. "Can't complain about that."

"Good point." He smiled and the whole world tilted on its axis. His face morphed to something more serious when he picked up the tablet, studied it, and then set it down again. "How well do you trust your security team?"

The question caught Kyra off guard. She'd trusted the men hired to protect her for the past few years without a blip. She wasn't putting it lightly when she said she trusted them with her life. The thought someone could betray her, her father, and their country sent a cold chill racing down her spine.

"They've been working for me a combined total of seven years," she stated a little more defensively than intended. "I'm related to one of them."

"I don't mean any disrespect," he said with a look of apology. "I'm just pointing out all the possible angles and trying to be as objective as I possibly can. Nothing personal to anyone who works to keep you safe."

She took in a deep breath before having another sip of coffee. This was hard to hear, let alone consider. But he was right to look at this from a fresh perspective.

"My cousin has been with me the longest," she began. "Five years to be exact, but I've known him my entire life. If he wanted to get back at me, he wouldn't have to set up this elaborate scheme. Plus, he doesn't want anything to do with the crown. Or at least he didn't the last time we spoke and I pitched the idea of him taking over someday for my father."

"Why would a criminal ring want to control your country specifically?" he asked.

"For starters, my father is getting older and has a heart condition. Not many people know this but he had a stroke last year. He's fine but naturally I'm worried about him," she admitted.

"I'm sorry," he said with a look in his eyes that said there was a story there.

"Thank you." She hadn't spoken those words out loud to anyone, and a little bit of the weight bearing down on her shoulders lifted.

"Crime rings want to control our banking system. Whoever is in charge can launder money through our country," she said. "My father can't change the system without losing support from the banks. It's a no-win situation on his side because the most logical step would be to close off the possibility."

"If something happens to your father, who wears the crown?" he asked, cocking his head to the side.

"That would be me," she admitted.

His gaze widened and that eyebrow shot up again. "Really?"

She nodded.

"Seems like a lot of responsibility for one person," he stated with more than a little shock in his voice.

She'd seen it before when she was in college and the question had come up, so it didn't catch her off guard. Being born into responsibility bigger than herself was a double-edged sword that had come with a lot of privilege and a whole lot of risk.

"It's just down to the two of us," she said. "Which won't matter if a criminal takes control of our country." She shuddered at the thought of her small country being subjected to people who would rob them blind and abuse a system that should protect them.

"Why take over your country at all?" he asked. "You're one piece of a bigger puzzle."

"That's simple. We're a gateway through Europe. It's easy to launder money through the person who controls the crown. They would also control law enforcement," she stated. "It's our weakness."

"Then, we're down to discussing your second personal security guard," he stated.

"Marko has been with me for the past two years and Pietro for longer than that," she said as he nodded. "He was carefully vetted by my father. There's history there."

"Okay." He picked up his cup of coffee and took a drink. He kept the cup at his lips and bit the edge a couple of times before setting it back down. "Who knew about the meetup point at the condo?"

"Only my security," she said on a sigh. They were going around in circles and the fingers kept pointing back to someone close to her. Impossible. Her cousin would no sooner trade her in than...hold on a second. Grayson didn't exactly say Zoya was responsible for giving away her location. "Are you thinking their cell phones might have been hacked?"

"I'm considering everything at this point. We find out how the condo information leaked and we start narrowing possibilities," he stated and his tone was unreadable.

"If it's safe here, why not stay?" She genuinely wanted to know.

"We will for the moment. Staying on the move is the only option. Moving targets are harder to hit." He shot a look she couldn't immediately discern. "Someone close to you knows where we are right now. I can't have that."

"Zoya?" Kyra didn't bother to hide her shock.

"I'm not saying she would give up your location on purpose," he quickly clarified. "It's dangerous for her and us for her to have that information when you're being hunted. Once we leave here, she no longer holds the key to finding you. That makes it safer for everyone involved."

"I can't argue your point there." Now that she understood his reasoning and had a decent night of sleep, she was ready to face their next move. "Any idea what that might be?"

"Our next move?"

She nodded.

"I haven't exactly nailed it down as of yet. There are a few ideas rolling around in my head," he stated.

"Let's hear them." She polished off the contents of the cup. "And please tell me they involve a strong cup of coffee."

Grayson picked up his cup and smiled. "I wouldn't exactly call this coffee. This is my third cup in a few hours and I feel nothing."

"Is it safe to go out? Tell me the truth," she urged, needing to assess their current level of risk.

"Right now, I believe so. But if someone got the information about your whereabouts from Zoya's phone, then they could hack into DNT—"

The look she shot him seemed to stop him midsentence.

"Dallas North Tollway," he clarified. "They have cameras at all toll booths."

"Which means they could have narrowed down our location," she stated.

"Exactly," he agreed with a hint of pride that she seemed to catch on so quickly.

"Staying seems dangerous. Leaving seems dangerous," she said on a sharp sigh.

"At this point, we're down to calculated risks," he pointed out.

"I'm sorry for putting you in danger," she said in all honestly. "I doubt you knew being with me was going to be this risky to your own life."

"The risk is mitigated," he said with a smirk. She must

have shot him quite the look because he added, "When you're as good as I am at staying alive."

"Thank you for sticking around then." She couldn't blame her friend for leaving but she'd also noticed how quickly Zoya took the out. "I'm not sure where I'd be without you."

"Based on what I saw at the condo, you'd be fine either way," he said with a wink that caused her stomach to free fall again. "But I'm still happy to be here and offer any help I can."

Why did those words mean so very much to her right now?

"I HAVE HALF a mind to take you back to my family's ranch." Grayson wasn't kidding either. There was security on the ranch. They could beef it up. But then he thought about all the discord on the ranch of late and all the threats they'd had.

Whether he wanted to entertain the idea or not, Kyra was already shaking her head.

"I won't put more people at risk than absolutely necessary," she said adamantly. "It's bad enough your life is on the line."

"Fair enough," he conceded. He could appreciate her for feeling the way she did. If given the same circumstance, he'd probably take the same approach. "No ranch."

"Okay," she agreed.

Ruling it out handicapped him because there were more ways than one to be on his family's land. One of which was camping.

"What about staying in Dallas?" she asked. "I mean,

won't everyone believe we took off and got as far away from here as possible?"

"Possibly," he stated. "What about your security team? How can we contact them?"

"There's a second location. Only my cousin knows about it," she told him. "We agreed to keep this one between us. If something happened and we couldn't meet at the condo last night, we would regroup in two days and meet up at Reunion Tower. There's a restaurant at the top of the ball and we planned to meet at the bar."

"Two days is nothing," he said and meant it. "I can keep us out of sight for forty-eight hours." He'd been on longer tracking missions than that.

"Perfect." Her eyes sparked and his heart took a hit. "First, better coffee. Maybe food that doesn't taste like the great outdoors. And more sleep."

"Sounds like a plan to me," he stated.

"Wait a minute, though. Did you sleep last night?" she asked.

"I don't need much. I napped for fifteen minutes here and there. It wasn't bad," he admitted. "Believe me, when I'm tracking a poacher I may go days without more than catnaps."

"This life you have on the ranch sounds interesting," she said, appreciation lighting her blue eyes. "I'd like to hear more about it."

"If waking up at four a.m. sounds appealing to you, then you might actually be fit for ranching," he joked.

"Be serious," she said with a smile that sent warmth spiraling through him.

"That is one hundred percent true," he said. "But the best part is being out on land that extends on farther than the eye can see and don't even get me started on the sky. It goes on for miles and miles. When the sun comes up it paints this amazing picture with more colors than a rainbow." He shook his head. "It's hard to explain just how majestic it all is when I'm outside and the land goes on for days, as does the sky. The feeling of being all alone in the world and yet not. I'm surrounded by so much life. When I'm out there I realize how small I am in comparison to the world." He glanced over at her a little embarrassed at droning on. "But, hey, it's probably not like that for everyone."

"Sounds like heaven to me the way you explain it," she said, her words connecting with a place deep inside his soul.

"I wasn't kidding about the early mornings. During calving season, my brothers and I have been known to fall asleep standing up, though," he said. "Long hours don't begin to describe what happens."

"What do you love the most about being a rancher?" she asked, and he liked the fact she wanted to know more about his world. He probably liked it a little more than was good for him.

"Being out on the land. The fact that no two days are alike. The freedom to really breathe," he said without hesitation. "I don't know how people survive in a concrete jungle. There are people everywhere but no one seems to stop long enough to really talk to one another. Neighbors don't know each other's last names, yet they practically live right on top of each other."

"It does seem strange to me how true that is," she seemed to agree. "I take it you know your neighbors."

"Not every single one of them, but it's hard not to know or at least have heard of families when you've spent your whole life in one place," he explained.

She nodded with a smile. "There is something very nice

about that. But it must also make meeting new people diffi-cult," she surmised. "How do young people stand it?"

"Austin is a young and vibrant city that's not too far away. Most of my youth was spent driving back and forth on week-ends," he said on a shrug. "Young people figure out a way."

"And now?" she asked with a nod of acknowledgment.

"It gets old after a while," he admitted. "Most people my age moved away a long time ago unless they have a family business that keeps 'em around and busy. The downside to being on a ranch with all that nature around is that having a serious relationship gets interesting."

Her eyebrows knitted together as she pulled her legs up and then hugged them to her chest.

"What I mean by that is being so busy all the time makes it difficult to spend the time with someone to get to know them. Things either have to move too fast, as in they live with you so you'll see each other on a regular basis, or be patient enough to take it slow and realize there'll be long stretches where I can't communicate depending on the time of the year," he clarified. Most of his relationships fell into the camp of moving too fast. At least until he'd learned his lesson. Moving Amy into his cabin had cured him of that when she'd tried to drive a wedge between him and his brothers by lying about them. In truth, she didn't want him around anyone else but her. Other jealous patterns emerged and he'd had a difficult time untangling the mess she'd made of a few of his relationships. Family always came first and any woman he dated needed to understand that.

"Dating can be tricky," she said on a sigh.

"Someone as beautiful as you shouldn't have a difficult time finding someone to go out with," he countered a little faster than he'd intended.

The red blush was back and it proved his point even

more. She was beautiful. But looks only got a person so far
in his book. Kyra was intelligent, had a sense of humor, and
he had all the respect for someone who knew how to hit a
mark with a metal star from a distance and under extreme
duress.

6

Kyra coughed to ease the dryness in her throat. There had never been a person in her life who caused her body to react in the same way when Grayson offered a compliment, let alone when he stood near her. Heightened emotions, she thought, deciding she needed to change the subject quickly.

"Think it's safe to get that strong cup of coffee now?" she asked, thinking a little caffeine could boost her heartrate and all that blood flow might help her think a little more clearly. As it was, she was getting lost in the fog that was Grayson Firebrand.

"Now that I think about it, I can probably have some delivered." He picked up the tablet. "Let me figure out how."

"Mind handing me your phone?" she asked, extending her arm toward him, palm facing up.

"All right," he said before meeting her halfway across the bed. "There you go."

Kyra took it. As she started tapping the screen, she realized she didn't have her belongings with her, which meant no money to pay for coffee. She blew out a breath and her shoulders slumped forward. This man had already done enough. It wouldn't be right to ask for more.

"Never mind the coffee," she said. "I'll drink what's already here."

Grayson had gone back to studying the tablet screen. He stopped what he was doing and looked over at her, really looked like he was trying to find the right word to fit into a crossword puzzle. And then something must have clicked in his mind because he nodded before reaching into his pocket and producing a wallet that he tossed onto the bed. It landed a few inches from her.

"Credit card is inside. I don't have it tied to my phone like most people. It just doesn't come in handy for me. I barely have a need to carry a wallet considering everyone in town knows me and can just bill the ranch," he said with one of those devastating smiles.

Kyra compressed her lips into a frown.

"I can't take advantage of your generosity," she finally stated. She felt firm on that point. Grayson Firebrand was already doing enough by feeding her and keeping her alive. She didn't have a right to ask him for a better cup of coffee too, no matter how good it sounded. And it sounded fantastic.

"I see," he said. "Then hand the phone over and I'll figure it out myself. But I plan on getting you a decent cup of coffee, because you deserve that much after everything you've been through. Plus, your mother must have been very close to mine if she's willing to send one of her sons to protect you. I can't have her thinking that I didn't use the good manners she brought me up with by not providing something besides this watered-down version of coffee. I don't even think there is real caffeine in here." His face twisted up like a skunk had just sprayed him.

She couldn't help but laugh.

"Only if you'll allow me to repay you once this whole ordeal is over or I am reunited with my wallet or security detail," she insisted. "But I have no idea how long that will take."

"We'll figure out something. Is that good enough?" he asked, looking like he had no intention of collecting.

Kyra nodded, satisfied she'd tried not to be a drain. The man had already put his life on the line for her and that went a long way in her book. Most of the people she came in contact with had their own ideas about who she was and how to treat her. The fact he'd believed her to be a maid when they first met probably took some of the edge off. Maybe?

"Did you really believe that I was a maid when we met in the condo?" she asked as she entered her drink order. She held a finger up. "Before you answer that, what do you want to drink?"

"Coffee. Strong. Black."

"Got it," she said, typing away in the local coffee shop's online menu. A delivery company would bring the drinks guaranteed to be fresh and hot, and on time according to their website promise. She'd had coffee delivery service in Canada before while staying at Zoya's house. It was extravagant and not something she would normally want to get in the habit of doing but decent coffee at this point was a necessity. It would help clear the cobwebs and kick her brain into high gear so she could think more clearly. She added a few pastries to the order so they wouldn't have to leave right away. They would be as comforting as the room she was in. There was something oddly familiar about being in this room. She'd couldn't remember the last time she'd slept so well or so deeply. Then again, Grayson had been here all night, awake, keeping vigilant watch. Her deep sleep probably had more to do with finally feeling safe.

"A proper cup of coffee will be here in ten minutes or less according to the app," she said proudly. She took note of the total and committed it to memory, making a personal promise to repay his kindness.

"That's impressive," he said with a smile. "Maybe I was too quick to judge city living. And, yes, you convinced me you were a maid. I didn't' have a whole lot of time to analyze the situation before we had to get out of there."

"Good point about needing a quick exit from the condo. And being able to order coffee definitely makes having one of those more useful." She motioned toward his cell. Rubbing her arms, she said, "I can't help but feel naked without mine." When she heard how that sounded, she corrected herself. "Lost is probably a better word."

The red blush crawling up her neck couldn't be helped. She'd never been able to hide her embarrassment easily. The same annoying reaction happened when she tried to stretch the truth too. It was probably a good thing Kyra wasn't a good liar. She might have gotten better at hiding many of her feelings over the years but the red blush had always been a dead giveaway.

"I've been going over the facts in my head all night," he said. "Of course, I'd like to speak to your security detail and your cousin. We'll know a whole lot more once we hear their version of the events and how this could have broken down."

"You made a good point about Zoya's cell phone earlier. It's common knowledge that we're best friends. Her making a sudden trip to Dallas from Vancouver could easily have tipped someone off. Why would she up and go somewhere there isn't an architectural site?" she reasoned.

"The easy answer usually is the right one," he admitted. "Two days we meet up with the others. Is there any way to get into contact with your cousin before then?"

"Not without risk," she said.

He seemed to consider options for a few seconds.

"I was thinking about buying a burner phone, but I can't be certain the location couldn't be traced. I'd have to figure out a way to divert the signal and make it seem like it was bouncing off a different cell tower," he stated.

"My cell was supposed to do that, but it seems difficult to stay one step ahead of technology advances. You know?" she asked, hoping he could relate.

"The minute we think we have a program or app that is secure, someone comes up with a counter to it," he agreed.

"Technology is out. Otherwise, you could just call my cousin. I know his number," she informed.

"By heart?" The look on Grayson's face was priceless.

"I was forced to memorize his cell as well as my security team's," she explained.

"Being able to make the call would certainly make life easier in the moment," he said before compressing his lips into a frown.

"If only it was that simple," she said on a sigh. Nothing in life seemed to be simple anymore. The only surprise was that she'd gone from being a carefree kid with no worries to a twenty-five-year-old adult on the run in what felt like the snap of a finger.

"What are you thinking?" he asked with an arched brow. She'd seen a similar look on his face when he was trying to read her expression.

"Just how much life has changed in a short time. How much certain events can rip you out of your comfort zone in a heartbeat. And how one day all childhood and childish ideas are stripped away. You realize there are really evil people in the world who would harm you or someone you love over ridiculous things like power and greed," she said, realizing once she'd started talking more things because crystal clear.

"I agree with everything you said," he stated after a thoughtful pause. "But I'd like to add to it, if that's okay with you."

"Please," she urged.

"There are really evil people in the world but they are small in number and they help me realize just how good the truly good people are," he said. "Power and greed are complicated friends. Greed makes any power you already have seem like never enough. It becomes a never-ending cycle. People who get caught up in it never win in the end. It consumes them, changes them, and then eventually chews them up and spits them out leaving nothing but sadness in their wake."

"It sounds like you have a lot of personal experience with this topic," Kyra noted.

"Recent experience," he said with a slight nod. "My grandfather suddenly passed away a few months ago and there's a large inheritance at stake."

"Money can complicate family relationships," she stated. "And I'm sorry about your grandfather. Were the two of you close?"

"Nothing should get in the way of family," he said with more than a hint of melancholy in his tone.

It only served to make Kyra want to know him even more. Was it risky to get too personal?

GRAYSON WONDERED how much he should spill about his family's complicated relationships. Where would he even start? "Let's see." He paused, trying to find the right words. When none came, he decided to go for it anyway, "I already told you that my grandfather died in an accident on the ranch."

She nodded, leaning toward him like she was really listening and wanted to hear more.

"My father and uncle have been sworn enemies almost from birth, and my grandfather has pitted them against each other at almost every turn. The way he divided the ranch and mineral rights put them even more at odds. We've only recently found out that my aunt was responsible for the last-minute will change that gave her side of the family anything at all. I'd like to say we've all been cooperating and trying to figure out a fair compromise but am ashamed to admit there's been nothing but bad will and fighting on both sides."

"I'm sorry," she said, and those two simple words were balm to a wounded soul. They were words both sides of his family needed to learn how to use.

"Thank you. You might be surprised to hear this, but it means a lot." His cell buzzed, interrupting the moment. He checked the screen.

"Coffee's here," he stated, figuring the interruption was about to be worth it in a few minutes. "It's at the front desk, so I'll run and grab it."

Kyra's gaze searched around and he realized she was looking for the weapon. He'd moved it to his duffel bag earlier. The metal butt stuck out from the holster he'd stuffed inside a side pocket. He retrieved the weapon and set it on the nightstand beside her.

"This what you're looking for?" he asked.

She nodded.

"I'll be right back." He made the trek down the hallway, passing a young couple with a toddler in between them. Each parent had a hand and would occasionally swing the little kid that was all angelic round face and toothy smile. Her laughter was like a bubble clinging to a breeze and he couldn't help but smile at the tot. He thought about his niece back at home and how much he needed to step up his game as an uncle. There was work to do when he got home. Work that seemed less daunting in Kyra's presence. Maybe it was the fact she'd only had her father to lean on, but she had a quality that made him *want* to fix things between the warring sides of his family when he got back home.

Grayson retrieved the coffees and bag of pastries from the front desk, taking note of the shift change. A younger woman barely old enough to have a job smiled at him from behind the counter as he turned to walk away. He dismissed her as a non-threat. He might not know everything in life, but he sure knew innocence when he saw it. Kyra had been right a few minutes ago. There were events in folks' lives that woke them up to the dark side of humanity. He'd been exposed to some of it early in life with his father's affairs and his grandfather's knack for covering them up in the name of keeping secrets to preserve the family name. Some of his brothers had been to hell and back over it. Grayson, being one of the younger of the nine, hadn't been exposed to it as much as the others. In some ways, his older brothers had offered a kind of buffer for him. He could only imagine the price they'd had to pay to absorb much of the pain.

The hallway was empty by the time he returned, but the image of the happy little family that had been there a few moments ago tugged at his heartstrings. It was probably all the new couples at the ranch that messed with his mind and had him considering the unthinkable...what his own children would be like.

He set the drink tray down on the carpet while he fumbled with the keycard. Once the lock clicked, he opened the door enough to wedge a foot inside.

"It's me," he said so Kyra wouldn't shoot. He managed to pick up the drink tray with his free hand while gripping the pastry bag in the other and keep his foot in the door. This felt like an adult version of the game Twister.

"I can smell the coffee from here," Kyra said as he heard the sound of covers ruffling. She met him at the door as he stood up and regained his balance.

"Let me hold this for you," she said, grabbing the door.

He thanked her as he passed by. Her citrus scent overpowered everything else, washing through him. He cleared his throat before stopping at the small pull-out table and insisting she take the office chair this time. He'd seen the way she kept touching her back last night while sitting on the bed and figured she didn't want to complain. Sitting up like that killed the lower back. He should know after all the years he spent riding around in the back of a pickup truck as a kid. Of course, young people felt nothing compared to a person his age. At thirty-one, he was already starting to feel every ache and bruise that came with the hard work of ranching. Still, he wouldn't change his profession for the world. But he was probably going to have to start taking better care of himself if he wanted to last beyond age forty.

"This coffee is everything right now." Kyra made that same mewl of pleasure sound he'd heard before and it stirred his heart again just like it did last night.

Grayson took a sip of his.

"I couldn't agree more," he said as he pulled a blueberry muffin from the bag. He offered it to Kyra first before setting it on top of a napkin. The muffin was good sized and yet he polished it off in a few bites as Kyra took a Danish from the bag.

"Tell me more about your family, please," Kyra said.

He figured they had no answers in her case and a whole lot of time to kill. Why not? Plus, he surprised himself in actually wanting to talk more with her. "Okay. Well. Let's see. There has been a crime spree happening in Lone Star Pass since the death of my grandfather. Some of it is related to his death and part of it is unexplainable, except the old axiom, *when it rains, it pours*."

"Again, I'm so sorry about your grandfather," she repeated.

He acknowledged her sentiment with a nod. Her words meant a lot to him. "You asked about my relationship with him. To answer your question, no, we weren't close. Not as men, not as family, and not as people who lived on the same land. The only connection I've ever felt to him is his legacy. He loved Texas and the ranch with his entire soul. We are deeply bonded there, if that makes sense," he said, wondering how that sounded to someone else despite it making perfect sense to him.

"I understand better than you might think," she said, and there was something about the look in her eyes when she said that made him feel like she might be a kindred spirit.

"I've learned more things about him recently that are making me rethink how much I disliked him, but he doesn't deserve any medals for some of his behavior. Abusive childhood or not, he shouldn't have pulled some of the crap he did over the years, especially with my father and uncle," he continued.

She took another sip of coffee but gave rapt attention to

him as he spoke. Her eagerness to hear more kept him talking.

"We called him the Marshall growing up. Saying grandfather when referring to him just seems odd to me now," he continued. "But he had two sons who he pitted against one another for their whole lives, even to the day he died."

"That's so terrible," she said. He figured she might have a strong reaction considering all the family she had was her father. It was clear that she was close to her cousin, but it seemed like he was also the closest thing she had to a sibling. Grayson couldn't even imagine what that would be like. As much as he disliked the lack of privacy that was part of the deal with a large family, he wouldn't trade a day of his childhood or any one of his brothers.

"The Marshall's will divided up his assets in a way that would force my father and uncle to cooperate for my uncle to get any of his share. At least, that's what we believed at first. Now, we found a will that changes everything, giving control of the ranch, land, and mineral rights to my side of the family. My aunt apparently got into the Marshall's head, causing him to change the will a while back. She went to a dark place of greed to keep the original will quiet," he said. "Now, she's in jail. My uncle is beside himself and I can't even begin to imagine what my cousins must be going through."

"You haven't reached out to them?" she asked.

"No. A few left the property during a recent investigation. They've been suspects in recent cases and, despite being cleared, this situation doesn't exactly put them in a good light," he said. "Plus, I haven't spoken to many of them in a while despite living on the same ranch. Work never stops and they aren't involved on the cattle side of things."

"They don't want to be?" she asked.

"I've never asked," he admitted.

"Maybe you should," she said. Her words struck a nerve because he'd been blaming his uncle and cousins for the state of their relationship but what had he ever done to change it?

7

"It's none of my business," Kyra stated the second she saw how much her words seemed to strike a physical blow with Grayson. "Forget I said anything."

Grayson shook his head. "You're exactly right. I've been building up our lack of relationship in my mind to say it's their fault but I haven't exactly done anything to change it. My uncle must be beside himself to learn the lengths his wife would go to prey on his aging father. The will had to have been a crushing blow to Uncle Keif. I can't even put myself in the position of my cousins; a few of them have pitched in to work the ranch. They have their own barn and do their own thing. It's strange to realize we've been living on the same land and yet so far apart from each other. We avoid each other like the plague, which is strange because a few of us grew up very close."

"I spent most of my life wishing I had a sibling," Kyra said. "Having a cousin has been the next best thing but we didn't grow up in the same house. I spent a lot of time with a nanny since my father was busy. Family is important."

"Interesting how easy it can be to lose sight of what

really is important," he agreed. "For the record, I've always considered myself beyond lucky to have a big family despite our many flaws."

"I can imagine your holidays must have been much different than mine." She took a sip of coffee, enjoying the bold taste. "Tell me what yours were like."

"The smell of cinnamon apples and chocolate chip cookies filled the house. Baking happened all day with my mother and we'd clear a plate the second she filled it. She's famous for her meatballs, though. There was always a fresh batch around the holidays. She's Italian so the sauces she made were and are out of this world," he said, practically beaming. "She loves to cook so there's always something in the oven or on the burner."

"Your mother sounds like the kind of mother everyone wishes for," she said.

"That's probably true," he agreed. "I have no complaints there. She loved us more than we deserved most of the time. I see that now and would walk through fire for that woman."

Kyra couldn't help but feel a little melancholy when the subject of mothers came up in conversation.

"What about your father?" she asked.

"You know how they say opposites attract?" he asked.

Kyra nodded.

"That's certainly true in the case of her and my father." His blue eyes darkened at the mention of the man. "He was selfish where my mother was giving. He was cruel where my mother was kind. The worst part about him, I'm learning now, is just how badly he treated our mother. Especially when they were young. He cheated on her and hid secrets."

"Sounds awful to know that about your parents," she said, figuring no relationship was uncomplicated. Her own mother had lived in an arranged marriage, and yet from all accounts had found true love with Kyra's father. "How have you forgiven him?"

"I'm not real sure that I have or ever will," he stated with a sadness in his voice that tugged at her heart.

"Has she been able to forgive him?" she asked.

"I believe so," he said. "She left him recently over something that bubbled up from the past, but then he had a stroke and now it's more than a little complicated."

"I'm so sorry, Grayson," she said.

"Thank you. He'll be fine but it did make me realize how much he loved my mother despite not being real sure of that in the past. They have their quirks as a couple, I'm certain of that, but they grew up in a time when the man went to work and the woman stayed home with kids. Lines were drawn that probably shouldn't have been and I can only imagine how terrible that could have been for a woman. Except that my mother seemed to love being home with us," he said. "She hummed when she worked in the kitchen and seemed to get great joy out of something as simple as feeding us. But she was modern too and could hold her own on any horse on the ranch."

"I've always looked at feminism as a stereotype. A group of people say we shouldn't like to cook because we're women and we only learned that role because we saw it." She blew out a frustrated breath. "Guess what? I like to cook too and I'm still a feminist. Cooking relaxed me. I also plan to have a career and maybe a husband and kids at some point but not if I don't meet the right person."

His eyebrow shot up again and she could see that her words resonated.

"I'd be perfectly happy as a single career woman. I don't need a relationship to define me. And yet, I could easily see myself deciding to stay home should I have children. I think of life as fluid and we need different things at different points in our lives. We don't know how we'll react to a situation until we're in it. You know?" she asked but he was already nodding.

"I've never seen myself as anything but a rancher. I doubt anything would ever change that for me, but my brother Adam has stepped back from ranch business quite a bit lately now that he has an infant daughter. He wants to be with her as much as humanly possible and to help his new bride. Babies are a ton of work but he's the happiest I've ever seen him," he said. "I don't think he would change a thing in his life and the ranch will always be there when he's ready to step up his responsibilities."

"It's wonderful he has that option," she said. "From what I know about my mother, she was put in a traditional role and there wasn't much wiggle room. Her marriage to my father was arranged but it turned out to be the real deal. I've been told she loved me more than life itself but she always wished to keep her career. It wasn't allowed."

"Women's minds are incredible. We need their intelligence and contributions to society in all areas. It's such a waste otherwise," he said, shaking his head. "There's no reason to pigeon-hole a person. Plus, there are plenty of working women who are also incredible mothers. And not every woman has to like to cook. They should only do it because they want to, not because they're forced."

Kyra liked his views. She also liked his intelligence and his passion when he talked about an injustice. Then again, there wasn't a whole lot that she didn't like about Grayson Firebrand.

"An arranged marriage?" he asked, circling back to their conversation a few moments ago.

"Afraid so," she admitted.

"And it worked out?" he continued.

"Seems so," she stated with confidence. Her aunt wouldn't lie about something so important, and neither would her father. She'd dismissed him at first because he'd lost his wife. Kyra thought he might be looking back at the marriage with rose-colored glasses. But her aunt on her mother's side, Charlie's mother had confirmed everything Kyra had been told.

"Interesting," he said.

"Care to explain?" she asked, unsure where he was going.

"You hear a whole lot about romantic love and end up convinced that's where it's at with relationships. You meet. You fall in love. Butterflies in the stomach and sweaty palms ensue. But what if we're looking at it all wrong? What if those butterflies are a warning and a sign that you've met *the one*?" he asked.

"If you can believe my father, he had butterflies the first time he put eyes on my mother," she said. "Their marriage might have been arranged but they got the final say. He seemed besotted with her based on the way he talks about her and I'm told the feeling was mutual."

"Score one for romantic love after all," he said with a smile that hit her in the center of her chest.

She glanced over at the clock and realized they'd been talking for hours. Being with Grayson had proved a much-needed distraction from real life. But time to get serious again was coming.

His cell phone had buzzed minutes ago and they'd been so involved in conversation that he hadn't checked it. As he picked up the phone, noise in the hallway caused her pulse to kick up a few notches.

Kyra reached for the gun on the nightstand as she

scooted out of bed. Instincts kicked in as she palmed the weapon, crossed the room, and moved to the door without making a sound. Grayson was beside her and his now-familiar spicy male scent filled her senses. A company could bottle and sell that scent, and make a fortune for the effect it would have on women.

She tilted her head up at him to look at him, considering he practically towered over her and she wasn't exactly considered short. Ear against the door, he slicked his tongue across his lips.

The commotion stopped in front of the door. And then a knock came. Kyra swallowed her scream as her hand came up to cover her mouth. Panic ratcheted her heartbeat up a few notches as a shot of adrenaline caused her hands to shake.

GRAYSON CHECKED the peephole and sighed relief when his brother Ian stood on the other side. "It's okay. He's family."

Kyra's huge eyes said she'd gone into a mild state of shock. She shook her head like she was shaking it off before holding up a finger. "Don't open until I'm in the bathroom, okay?"

"Sure," he whispered, figuring she would have to come out and meet his brother at some point.

She ran over to the bag and then darted into the bathroom. "Okay."

Grayson opened the door to his baby brother. Ian was twenty-eight, three years younger than Grayson. He brought Ian into a bear hug.

"What are you doing here?" Grayson asked as he checked the hallway then ushered Ian inside the room.

"Checking on you," Ian said. He might be a little green behind the ears and the brother no one took too seriously but he had a heart of gold and was wise beyond his years. He glanced around the room, clearly looking for Kyra. Their mother must have filled him in.

"Are you here as my replacement?" Grayson asked. The thought of stepping away from the assignment now was unthinkable.

"Mom did say she forced you into this," Ian admitted. He had a duffel bag strapped to his back that he shouldered off.

"Take a seat," Grayson said, motioning toward the office chair.

"No, thanks. I've been sitting for hours. I'd rather stand if that's okay with you," Ian said, moving toward the glass doors leading out to the patio. He pulled the curtain back enough to let sunlight in. "Is this okay?"

"Fine with me." Grayson enjoyed the sunshine. This place had been like a cave without the curtain cracked open. It was dangerous to open too far, though.

"Where is...?"

And then it dawned on Grayson. His brother wasn't here because he happened to be in the neighborhood running an errand. Dallas was hours away from Lone Star Pass. Ian had been sent to give Grayson an out if he wanted to ditch the assignment.

"Kyra is in the bathroom," Grayson said. "I think having someone show up out of the blue scared her."

"I apologize for coming here unannounced. I really did have business in Dallas, so Mom thought it would be a good idea if I stopped over and got a barometer on how it was going," he stated. "And before you ask what business I came here for, I'll be honest and say it wasn't anything that couldn't be handled over the phone. Business was an excuse."

"Your honestly is much appreciated," Grayson said.

"Let's hope I didn't scare the princess off too much," Ian said, glancing around again.

The covers on one bed were tussled and his brother seemed to take note of the fact the other bed hadn't been touched.

"I didn't sleep last night," Grayson said with a yawn. "Are you heading back right away?"

"No rush on my part," Ian said.

"Cool. Mind if I grab a couple hours of shuteye once I introduce you to Kyra?" Grayson asked, figuring as long as his brother was here, he might as well be put to work.

"Not at all. I'm here to help in any way that I can," Ian said as he rested his hands on his hips. "By the way, how serious is the situation?"

"We got chased out of a condo last night almost the minute I arrived," Grayson stated.

"That doesn't sound good," Ian said.

"I need to circle back to the cops and explain or they'll be looking for us too," Grayson said. "Actually, Kyra wanted to do that. Now that you're here, I can get a few other things done that I couldn't think of before. How long did you say you could stick around?"

"As long as you need me to," Ian said. "In fact, I can take over for you at any point if you need to head home."

"No, no. I don't want to abandon Kyra," he said quickly. A little too quickly?

"Okay, that's a fair point," Ian said as he turned to study his brother.

"She's been through a whole lot recently and I'd like to see this through to the end when she can go back to her country safely and her father is returned to power," Grayson explained. He realized that overexplaining made him seem guilty of something.

"It's understandable after what you must have gone through together last night," Ian said.

Grayson nodded, realizing his feelings probably went a little deeper than that. "It's serious. Someone came after her with either the intention of kidnapping her or killing her. Whoever is behind this coup attempt is covering all bases and seems to think if they get ahold of her, they can get to her father."

"A daughter would be any man's weak spot. I've seen it with Adam now that he has Angel," Ian said. "Precisely the reason I only plan to have boys." He laughed and Grayson had to take a second to get over the shock of his baby brother thinking about becoming a father someday.

"Since when did you become such a grown-up?" Grayson teased. He couldn't fathom Ian as a bona fide adult, but it was probably time to look at him in a new light as the man he'd become.

"About the time everyone around me started getting married," Ian said with a chuckle.

"Sounds like you've thought about fatherhood since before summer," Grayson said.

"True," Ian admitted. "I guess I've always known that I want to have a house full of boys like we did. You have to admit our childhood wouldn't have been the same without each other."

"No, it would not," Grayson agreed.

"Don't you think about having a wife and kids some-day?" Ian turned the tables.

"Not really," he said. "The thought never appealed. Too much responsibility, I guess."

"No one is ever ready for that part," Ian said.

"Since when did you become more mature than your older brothers?" Grayson asked, only half kidding.

"I had no choice," Ian quipped. "All of my brothers are older than me and someone has to lead the way."

"Funny," Grayson said as the bathroom door opened. He looked at his brother and whispered, "Are you ready to meet a princess?"

Ian compressed his lips then broke into a smile. "Why not?"

8

Kyra had changed into the athleisure outfit of leggings, sports bra, and tank top that Grayson had ordered for her. These clothing items came in sizes that left a lot of room for error. Grayson had absolutely nailed it.

"Kyra, this is my brother Ian," Grayson said as she entered the room.

"Nice to meet you," she said before walking across the room and offering a handshake.

"I'm not sure if I should bow or leave it at a handshake," Ian said with a grin that reminded Grayson of what his kid brother looked like in high school. The two of them didn't have too many years in between them.

"Handshake is good enough for me," Kyra said with a warm smile that seemed to put Ian at ease almost immediately. He'd noticed the soothing effect she'd had on Zoya as well. Was this part of her royal upbringing? Learning how to calm everyone and make them feel seen and heard? It seemed easy for her to slip into the role of princess. Even in workout clothing, she seemed dignified and carried herself with a certain elegance.

Who was there to calm her when she needed it?

"My brother came to help out in any way possible," Grayson said.

"Thank you," Kyra said before perching on the edge of the bed where she'd slept last night.

"While he's here, I'll grab a few hours of shuteye," Grayson stated. "Before I power down, is there anything you need?"

"Lunch would be nice if it's not too much trouble," Kyra said with the warm smile that stirred something inside Grayson's chest.

"No trouble at all," he said without hesitating.

"I can run out and grab anything that sounds good," Ian offered. He held out his cell phone. "If you want to find a place and check out the menu, I'll place the order and pick it up."

Kyra looked to Grayson, who nodded. She took the cell phone as Grayson excused himself to the bathroom. He washed his face and brushed his teeth. By the time he returned, Kyra had settled on shrimp tacos from a local and, apparently highly regarded, taco shop.

"Do you want anything?" she asked. "Ian already put his order in."

"Grab me whatever you're having," Grayson said. "I'll eat when I wake up."

Kyra nodded before tapping the phone's screen. She glanced up with a smile before handing the cell back to his brother. "There you go."

"Cool." Ian took the offering. "I'll run out and grab the order. Anything else you need while I'm out?"

"We could use more power bars and waters," Grayson

said. "A few snack items might be nice for Kyra to have around. Breakfast bars. Whatever you think we can use. Oh, and a burner phone would be nice."

"You got it," Ian said without hesitation. "How many days am I covering for food?"

"Just today and tomorrow," Grayson said, figuring the meetup with Charlie and the security team could be a game-changer. "We have a meeting in a day and a half that will determine our next steps."

"But any idea how many days this whole situation could last?" Ian continued. It was a fair question. There was just no real answer to it.

"Not at this time," Kyra answered. "My father could step back into power at any moment and this will all be set aside. All it takes is for him to gain the right allies, which I'm certain he's working on at this very minute. No one wants peace in Serentia more than my father. He has devoted his entire life to the people and has said he will go to his grave taking care of them."

"He sounds like an honorable person," Grayson said. His compliment was met with a genuine smile from Kyra.

"I think so," she said.

"In the meantime, it sounds like I need to rally three to four days' worth of basics," Ian stated.

"Just like when we go after a poacher," Grayson said.

"Got it. On it," Ian said before heading toward the door. "I brought a few more supplies from home in case they're needed. Pick through the duffel and take what you can use."

Grayson nodded.

"Take a key and knock three times fast, three times slow so we know it's you," Grayson said to his brother.

"Just like the treehouse," Ian said, and Grayson's heart

swelled that his brother remembered their signal from childhood.

"That's right," Grayson said as his brother headed out the door. He walked over to the made bed and practically threw himself on top, repositioning the pillows to get more comfortable.

"This might sound like an odd question. Feel free to say no," Kyra said, all the confidence stripped from her tone all of a sudden.

"Ask me anything," he said. "Nothing is off the table."

"Can I join you over there?" she asked. Her question caught him off guard.

It only took a second or two to recover. He lifted the cover.

"Come on over," he said, figuring she needed the reassurance more than anything else. She most likely wanted a warm body next to hers and the comfort of lying beside him. So, he wouldn't read too much into it.

Kyra slipped under the covers and turned her back to him, facing the window. She scooted back until they were body-to-body. And then she turned around and repositioned herself into the crook of his arm.

"Thank you," she whispered before closing her eyes.

"Any time," he responded, hearing the huskiness in his own voice. He couldn't deny the way she fit him so perfectly or how amazing her body felt against his. All that was between them was a little bit of cotton and denim. So, sleeping was probably going to be next to impossible when she was this close. Too many other things came to mind that he'd like to do with her. Stuffing those thoughts down, he held her closer.

A few minutes later, her even, steady breathing said she'd gone to sleep. He must've nodded off too, because the next thing he knew there were three fast knocks followed by three slow ones. The snick of the lock came next and the sound of the door opening.

Kyra sat bolt upright and her hand immediately flew to the nightstand. Grayson sat up too, noticing that her eyes were still closed. He gently guided her back down as he said a few reassuring words.

"Food's here," Ian stated as he bolted the door behind him.

"Shhhh," Grayson said as he peeled himself out of the covers and then scooted to the edge of the bed. "She fell asleep."

"I thought you were the one who was tired," Ian said in a whisper as he set the bag of tacos down on the pull-out table.

"She hasn't slept much since this whole ordeal began a week ago," Grayson explained.

His brother's eyebrow shot up and a question was written all over his expression. *How do you know what she has and hasn't done?*

"We had all of last night and all morning today to get me up to speed on what's been happening and how she ended up in this situation," he said by way of defense. "She admitted that sleep has been rare and she has been through hell and back trying to escape her country on a moment's notice. It's actually pretty unbelievable she's made this far."

"She sounds like a survivor," Ian said as he rolled the table toward Grayson.

"You can say that again," Grayson agreed. "If someone had told me this type of thing was still happening in our modern world, I would have told them to put the funny pipe down."

"It does sound like fantasy when you really think about

it," Ian said, setting the makeshift table up with food and drinks. He'd set another couple of bags down next to the dresser on his way in. Those must contain the supplies they would need to get through the next few days.

"I can say one thing is certain. She isn't at all what I expected. And I mean that as a compliment," Grayson said to his brother as they each picked up a taco.

"Never thought I'd see the day either of us would be here with a princess wearing athleisure wear," Ian said with a chuckle.

"Life can be strange," Grayson agreed.

"But those unexpected parts can be the best too," Ian pointed out. "Look at Adam and Prudence. Don't even get me started on Angel. Who would have thought our big brother would step into the role of husband and father so easily?"

"Not me," Grayson admitted. "Not in a million years."

"Agreed." Ian polished off one taco before picking up a second.

"He's the happiest I've ever seen him though," Grayson said before finishing his taco.

"Then there's Brax and Raleigh Perry," Ian said as Kyra stretched out her arms and yawned.

"Is that food I smell?" she asked, and her sleepy voice tugged at Grayson's heart. He realized he was falling down a slippery slope of attraction—an attraction he couldn't rein in if he tried.

"It sure is," he said. "Sit up and eat whenever you're ready."

"It smells way too good not to eat while it's fresh." She sat up and then scooted to the edge of the bed beside Grayson. Their outer thighs touched and electricity charged through him.

Ian shot a warning glance. Had he picked up on the chemistry between Grayson and Kyra? Would it bother Grayson if his brother had?

"I NEVER KNEW a shrimp taco could be this amazing." Kyra polished off two and downed half her Coke in a matter of minutes. The tacos were beyond good and she had no idea what kind of sauce was used. All she knew for certain was that she wanted more now.

"Texas has Tex-Mex food down to a science," Grayson said. "On the rare times I go into a bigger city, it's what I consider the best part of the trip."

"With food like this, who would ever leave?" she quipped, thinking how true that absolutely was. She'd grown up with cooks and, granted, the food was always good. Not exactly gourmet but it got the job done. Her father's taste buds had always leaned toward the bland side despite hiring chefs from the best culinary schools. It wasn't until college that she'd discovered Tabasco and then Sriracha. There'd been no going back after a couple of dabs from one of those bottles.

"Texas could always use a few more princesses," Ian chimed in.

"Do you have others?" Kyra asked, and her brow shot up. She was genuinely curious.

"Not actual princesses like you, but a whole lot of people who believe they are," Ian said with a smile.

Kyra laughed. It felt good.

"I wonder how many would want the title if they knew what it really came with," she said, rolling her eyes and smiling. Smiling was the best tension breaker and she genuinely needed a break from being on the edge of her seat. Being with Grayson was the first time she'd really slept. With him around, she could fall asleep at the drop of a hat and drop it herself. Now that his brother was here, she felt even safer.

"I've lived in Texas my entire life and haven't seen one person, man or woman, who can throw a star like you," Grayson said. "It isn't just your crown that makes you special. You have a unique ability to keep cool in pressured situations."

"Thank you." The red blush was back, creeping up her neck again. She wished she didn't give away her emotions so easily. She cleared her throat and took another sip of Coke. "We have some time to kill. Tell me more about your family."

Ian smacked his hands together. "This ought to be good."

"Growing up with nine boys under one roof was fantastic if you don't mind your legs being snapped by towels until they practically bled," Grayson said with a chuckle. His eyes lit up every time he spoke about his brothers. "This guy right here shared a bathroom with me. He was the world's worse when it came to snapping a towel."

"What does that mean exactly?" she asked.

Ian's jaw almost dropped to the carpet. "You've never been snapped by a towel?"

"Afraid not," she admitted. "I went to an all-girls school. We had strict rules about how we behaved with each other."

"Hold on." Ian hopped up and disappeared in the bathroom. He returned with one of the white bath towels, holding onto one corner as the rest of it fell out of its neat fold. "First, you hold onto opposite corners. Then, you twirl. Then...snap." He flicked his right wrist while letting go of the backend of the towel he'd been holding in his left hand. The towel made a snapping noise before the backend tapped the wall.

"That looks like it would hurt," Kyra said.

Ian pursed his lips together and nodded. "That's the whole point."

Grayson laughed, and it was a low rumble in his chest. "Keeps you on your toes, that's for sure."

"I've been around boys playing sports and seen the way they tease each other," she said.

"Imagine that twenty-four-seven for your entire child-hood and high school years," Grayson said.

She must have made quite the face because both men started laughing.

Once the laughter settled, Ian became serious. "Have you been by to see our father yet?"

Grayson shook his head. "You?"

9

Grayson didn't want to air *all* the dirty laundry about his family in one evening but he did feel like him and Kyra had grown closer in the short time they'd spent together. It made him think he owed her an explanation as to why he wouldn't go see his own father after being released from the hospital after having a stroke.

"I swung by before I came here," Ian said. "Mainly to check on Mom but he was there. Obviously."

"And? How did he look?" Grayson had good reasons for not visiting. At least, they'd seemed like good reasons up until now. Now, he was beginning to think they fell into the category of petty excuses.

"His face was a little bit ashen, and he hasn't been eating as well. It's surprising how much weight someone can drop in a short time," Ian admitted.

"But he looked good otherwise?" Grayson's curiosity was piqued. Before, it was easy to ignore his father's condition or what the man might look like after the stroke. Talking about him made it all that much more real that his father was never going to be the same again.

"Mom is taking excellent care of him," Ian said. "Not that he deserves her."

"That's one hundred percent fact," Grayson stated. Out of the corner of his eye, he saw Kyra studying him. He could only wonder what was going on in her mind. She would give anything to be with her father again, to know that he was alive and well, and to see him back on the throne. Grayson's relationship with his own father was more complicated. It wasn't that he wished the man harm or anything along those lines. He did, however, have a difficult time facing a weakened version of someone who had always been the epitome of strong. Grayson also needed to air out his feelings toward his father and didn't want to send the man back into another stroke.

"He's different now," Ian said.

"How so?" Grayson figured as much. There was no way someone could have a stroke and not be affected. Their father wasn't old by any stretch of the imagination but he wasn't young any longer either. Ranch work was physically challenging for younger, stronger folks.

"It's all in the way he looks at Mom now," Ian said. "I can't put my finger on it exactly but he seems to know what he almost lost."

Grayson turned to Kyra. "Not only did my father have affairs when our parents were younger, but one produced a child who my mother took to raise. His own mother died during childbirth and ours took him in as one of her own. She couldn't have loved him any more if he'd been flesh and blood."

"I always thought she favored Brax growing up," Ian admitted.

"We all did," Grayson said. "So much is explained now."

"And your mother took this child in?" Kyra seemed a little stunned.

"She did. The way she saw it was that Brax was our half brother and belonged on the ranch. He didn't have a mother so she took him to raise without a second thought," Grayson stated.

"Your mother sounds like an amazing human being," Kyra said, the admiration in her voice resonated with Grayson. Hell, he looked at his mother in much the same way. The woman was a saint as far as he was concerned, and that was long before he was told she'd taken Brax to raise as her own, knowing full well her own husband had had an affair.

Grayson and Ian both nodded.

"Your father sounds like a man with many regrets," she surmised after a thoughtful pause.

"I couldn't tell you," Grayson said.

"That is right on point with what I saw in his eyes," Ian said.

Grayson couldn't imagine the kind of pain that came with a cheating spouse. He had enough trust issues as it was. He and his father hadn't been close while he was growing up. He and the Marshall weren't exactly fishing buddies. Grayson was, however, close to his mother and brothers. A couple of his cousins came to mind. Him and Tanner were the same age and had been in the same grade in school. They played on the same sports teams and had buddied around a lot when they were young. When did all his relationships with his cousins sour? Had Aunt Jackie been pitting them against each other all of this time?

"After Adam and Prudence took over the main house, I couldn't help but wonder how the other side of the family felt about it," Grayson said to his brother. "I know the will gave our side everything but the houses where they lived and the plots of land where their houses were built. But wouldn't they want a piece of the Marshall's home?"

"I guess no one ever thought to ask," Ian admitted. "At least, I can speak for myself when I say that."

"It must have been hard on them, watching us take possession of everything," Grayson said.

"The Marshall was clear in his will. And yet, I can't help but think we were jerks not to take our cousins' feelings into consideration," Ian said.

"Honestly, I'm sick and tired of all the fighting. I have never cared one way or the other who gets what at the ranch. All I care about is continuing to do what I love," Grayson said with a little more heat in his voice than he'd intended.

"You won't get any argument from me. I always believed we should toss the will in the trash and just split everything down the middle. The Marshall created enough division in the family during his lifetime. He shouldn't get to do the same thing in death," Ian said, and Grayson couldn't agree more.

Of course, none of it was as simple as that. For starters, it wasn't their call to make. Their father would have to make that decision.

"Now that Aunt Jackie is behind bars for attempted murder, the family has grown even further apart," Grayson said, shooting a quick glance at Kyra to see how she reacted to the revelation. She locked eyes with him and there was such understanding in her gaze.

"Have you reached out to anyone on the other side yet?" Ian asked.

Grayson shook his head.

"I have no idea what to say," Grayson admitted. "And I

can only imagine what Fallon and Birdie are going through after learning our aunt tried to kill Birdie and her sweet Meg." He looked to Kyra when he said, "Birdie is my brother Fallon's new bride and Meg is her grandmother." He shot a look of apology. "My family must sound pretty out there to someone like you."

"We might not fight within our family but we do in our nation, and that's pretty much the same thing. An evil person is trying to take over and take control of our small country for his own greed," she said. "I can't imagine how awful it would feel if that person turned out to be a relative."

Grayson caught her gaze and held it. The unspoken words between them were clear as day. They didn't know who was behind the coup attempt yet and he wouldn't rule anyone out, not even her cousin. Even she had to admit he would have access to her friend's cell phone number.

She gave a small headshake as though she could read his thoughts. Or maybe she was trying to convince herself it wasn't possible. He couldn't blame her.

Kyra wasn't ready go there with Charlie. He'd been too much like a big brother for her to believe he could turn on her family. There was no amount of money that would entice him. Period.

"Family can be a real blind spot," Ian said, and his words were the equivalent of a hammer being slammed into her head.

"Promise me you'll look at the problem from all angles," Grayson said quietly.

She took a few seconds to breathe before giving a slight nod. Despite not believing Charlie would ever do anything to hurt her personally, he could possibly be tricked into doing it without realizing what was happening. Mistakes were made. The wrong people were trusted sometimes. "I'll keep my eyes wide open no matter who I'm around."

"That's all I'm asking," Grayson said.

"Why do I think this conversation is no longer about our family?" Ian asked. He deserved to know, so Grayson provided the short version.

"As much as I can't fathom my own cousin betraying us, after hearing about your family I'd be naïve to close my eyes to the possibility," Kyra said. "I would like, however, it to be noted that I don't believe Charlie is knowingly involved in hurting my family. Anyone can be tricked."

"Duly noted," Grayson agreed. He also realized that his cousins might have had nothing to do with their mother's crimes. But then, any one of them could have reached out by now. None had. He turned to Ian. "Why do you think the other side has been so quiet?"

"Considering our mother would never do something so evil, it's impossible for me to understand what our cousins might be going through in all this," he said. "We know Kellan has been in a feud with Corbin over Liv, so it's no surprise he hasn't made contact."

"Not to mention him and Adam are like gasoline on fire," Grayson pointed out.

Ian nodded. He picked up a Coke and set it down before taking a sip.

"Did you ever get the rest you needed?" Ian asked.

Grayson shook his head. "I got a second wind when the food came."

"Why don't you grab some shuteye then? You'll rest better on a full stomach," Ian suggested.

"I might conk out for a little while too," Kyra said, stretching her arms and yawning. "Mind if I stay over here?"

Her question, directed at Grayson, elicited a look from Ian. This wasn't the time to discuss the fact he was only consoling a woman who'd been scared out of her gourd. She was seeking comfort and that was all. Any decent person could be substituted in Grayson's place. A little voice in the back of his head picked that moment to point out how much his own comment stung. Was it so wrong he wanted to be different—special?—in the princess's eyes?

Different time. Different place. This whole scenario might go down in a different way.

"Be my guest," Grayson said to Kyra. "The bed's big enough for two." Grayson immediately acknowledged that was about the lamest thing he could have said right now. With a headshake, he moved on and hoped everyone else in the room did too.

"I may change and go for a run," Ian said. "If no one minds me making a little noise going in and out."

"All good here," Grayson said, thankful his brother seemed ready to let the other comment slide.

"Just open your eyes before you shoot when I come back," Ian said with a smile. Based on the flash of wariness in his eyes, he was only half joking. Accidents accounted for far too many deaths involving guns.

"We'll be careful," Grayson reassured.

Ian moved to the bathroom with his duffel, presumably to change out of the jeans and black t-shirt he'd shown up in. He toed off his boots next to the dresser on his way. Kyra wasted no time climbing under the covers, so Grayson joined her. She immediately reclaimed her spot from earlier. Being this close to her reminded him just how long it had been since he let anyone in. He'd dated over the years but the shine of a new relationship prospect had worn off long ago. The fact his baby brother had already considered getting married and having kids someday had been a real shock to Grayson's system. Shouldn't he be ready for those things? Shouldn't he be thinking about how nice it might be to have a family?

Was there something wrong with him that he didn't?

"I'll be back soon," Ian said softly from the short hallway. He didn't reappear in the room and Grayson let the comment go without a response. Instead, he pulled Kyra a little closer thinking how she deserved all those things and so much more.

Grayson closed his eyes, breathing in the citrusy scent and feeling the warm body that was a perfect fit. It would be so easy to get lost in the woman beside him. The next time he opened his eyes, Ian sat on the chair reading on the iPad. A corner lamp lit the room in a soft glow. Grayson was shocked he'd fallen asleep, even for a little while.

Kyra's steady, even breathing said she was still asleep. Slowly, he extricated himself from the tangle their arms and legs had become. Ian glanced up from the iPad, gave a small nod and a smile.

"I'm seeing some pretty big players going after her father," Ian whispered as Grayson made coffee.

He nodded and then offered the first cup to his brother.

"Thank you," Ian said, taking the cup.

"My biggest concern is how did they get to her." Grayson relayed the story of her escape to a wide-eyed brother.

"That's the kind of stuff you'd expect to see in a thriller movie, not real life," Ian said, clearly in awe.

"She's been trained in martial arts and is half the reason I'm sitting here in front of you right now instead of..." He let his voice trail off instead of going into those details with his brother. "Let's just say she's amazing on many fronts and I'm grateful for her training."

"But you think this is an inside job," Ian surmised.

"The way her location was found out here in Dallas," he began, "it's the only thing that makes sense."

"And the three people closest to her, besides her friend Zoya, are Marko, Pietro, and Charlie," Ian continued.

"That's right," Grayson stated. "It could be what we've been through recently with our family but I keep going back to the cousin."

"Why is that?" Ian asked.

"A gut feeling and nothing more," Grayson stated with a shrug.

"Our family history might be influencing you there," Ian said.

"You might be one hundred percent right," Grayson agreed. "It's next to impossible to separate the two from each other."

Ian nodded before taking a sip of coffee.

"I've been thinking about reaching out to Tanner," Grayson admitted. "He's been on my mind since our conversation earlier."

"Sounds like a good idea and might go a long way toward healing this family," Ian said.

"It's bizarre, isn't it? We all started off as friends years ago," Grayson said. "With the exception of Adam and Kellan. Those two were born fighting." Grayson quirked a smile.

"Agreed," Ian said. "But I think I know what you mean. Life got complicated and now Corbin and Kellan are in a standoff with each other over Liv."

"She and Corbin belong together," Grayson stated. "Everyone knows that."

"Tell that to Kellan's heart," Ian pointed out.

"True. There couldn't be much worse than seeing someone you love married to someone else every day of your life." Grayson hadn't really thought about it from his cousin's perspective. Granted, Kellan shouldn't have pursued Liv in the first place, considering she'd been Corbin's best friend since forever. But his brother had been engaged to another woman when Kellan asked Liv out. "The whole situation is messy."

"You could say that again," Ian quipped. "Wouldn't you say that describes our entire situation with the family at this point?"

Grayson nodded.

"Even if our father did the right thing and split the ranch, there are still mineral rights to consider. Would Uncle Keif be willing to give those up?" Ian asked.

"I doubt he has a choice now with the new will," Grayson said.

"True." Ian nodded. "I still think we should do the right thing and split everything down the middle. There's enough for everyone."

"Actually, little brother, you just made me look at this situation in a whole new light," Grayson said. "I kept wondering how we would split everything down the middle and still get along. Let's face it, our father and uncle can't agree on much so I can't fathom them trying to run a business together. But then, what you just said made me realize I've been looking at it all wrong. Why not have Firebrand Ranch V1 and V2? Our father can keep the original logo and Uncle Keif can use a V2 stamp or something to differentiate between the two. They both benefit from the Firebrand name."

Ian was already nodding before Grayson finished.

"There's no reason the cattle can't be split down the middle too. They're all tagged so the allotment could be randomized," Ian said, holding up the iPad.

"Exactly," Grayson said.

"Problem is, the others might not see it the same way and everything is ultimately up to our father," Ian pointed out.

Grayson figured it would be easier to milk a frog than get both sides of his family to agree on splitting up the ranch. He was frustrated with the situation and with himself. Him and his brothers had stood to the side and watched their father and uncle disagree, draw lines in the dirt, and be awful to each other far too long. They had no right to complain about a situation they weren't trying to change. It made them just as guilty as far as he was concerned. He needed to do better and he would.

10

K yra stretched out her arms and felt around for Grayson beside her. Instead of his warm body and spicy male scent she got cold sheets. She blinked her eyes open and searched for the source of hushed voices.

Grayson and his brother sat across from each other, quietly talking in the corner of the room. The resemblance between brothers was remarkable. Both were ridiculously tall, well over six feet. They were more like six-feet-four-inches if she had to guess. The average height of men in her country was five-feet-ten-inches and most seemed to ride the line. These guys had half a foot on the men back home. Height was one thing but stacked muscles seemed to be another family trait. She figured those came both naturally and from the amount of physical labor they performed in a day. There didn't seem to be the need for gyms or personal trainers on a ranch.

They both had dark hair, with Grayson's being a tad lighter with a few more blond streaks. Both had faces carved from granite but Ian's jaw was far more squared. And then there was Grayson's eyes. Eyes with the softest, bluest irises surrounded by a sea of white. Don't even get her started on his thick lashes. The five-o'clock shadow gave his face an edge but she could get lost in those eyes for days.

Both men would be considered smokin' hot by most standards but there was something extra special about Grayson in her book. His sex appeal drew her in and made her want to push up to her tiptoes and press a kiss to those lips of his that formed a bow.

Kyra cleared her throat so as not to surprise either one of them.

"Hey," Grayson said, his deep timbre sending a sensual current rippling through her. So much for keeping it cool.

"I can't believe how much I've slept in the past twenty-four hours," she said, pushing up to sitting.

"That's good. I can't imagine how tired you must have been after what you've been through," Grayson said as Ian nodded. He picked up the iPad and studied the screen.

"This is the first time in a long time that I've been able to let my guard down around people," she admitted. "I owe you both a huge thanks for that." Despite only knowing both of them for a matter of hours, she knew instinctively they were people she could trust. Within moments of meeting Grayson, she'd felt a connection. Her sense of trust with Ian came by extension of the bond formed with his brother.

"That's good to hear," Grayson said, and yet an emotion flashed behind his eyes that she couldn't quite pinpoint. Disappointment?

No. Couldn't be. She was clearly seeing things that weren't there. Sleep deprivation and stress would do that to anyone. Plus, she'd had to run a mental list of everyone close to her, then pick apart every relationship looking for a possible weak link, looking for someone in her inner circle who would betray her.

"Coffee?" Grayson asked, motioning toward the machine. "Or should I say dirty brown water?"

They both laughed and it was so nice to have a break from the stress if only for a few moments here and there. She would take what she could get and run with it.

"I would love a cup," she said. "But I don't mind making it."

"Don't worry about it," Grayson said. "It's no trouble and it gives me something to do with my hands."

She nodded, not wanting to think about what those hands could do to her body under the right circumstances. The thought of his hands, rough from work, against her skin sent more of those currents rippling through her.

"Perfect," she said, and she could hear the frog in her throat. The red blush was back too, a curse that came with a fair complexion.

"We should talk about the meetup tomorrow at Reunion Tower," Ian interjected.

"Good idea," Grayson said a little too quickly.

"I have the area pulled up on the map here." Ian held up the screen and tilted it toward Kyra. She crossed the room and sat on the edge of the other bed in time to be handed a cup of coffee.

"Will you be staying on through tomorrow night?" she asked Ian.

"Yes, ma'am," he said before glancing up and twisting his face into an apology. "I should probably say, Your Highness."

She swatted a hand in the air. "Please. Don't. I get enough of that back home and all I ever did to deserve it was being born."

Both the Firebrand men laughed.

"We know what that feels like," Grayson said.

"Blessing and a curse all wrapped up in one," Ian agreed.

Coming from cattle ranching royalty in a state like Texas made her realize just how much they actually had in common. All three were born into their families and had no say in the matter. All three had incredible advantages because of it. And all three had their own struggles in life that came with being in the public eye.

She was beginning to see why her connection to Grayson was so strong. Kindred spirits? Twin souls? It wasn't lost on her that she didn't feel quite the same bond with his brother. With Ian there was more mutual understanding than anything else. Either way, she appreciated both of them. Even her own family never understood her position or the fact she wanted to make her own way in life, rather than ride on her father's coattails. The need to be her own person and not shaped into something she wasn't, had been born inside her too. Kyra wondered how many of those qualities came from her mother.

"What about your grandparents?" Grayson asked. "Are you very close with either side?"

"Me? No," she said. "My mother's parents died before I was born. On my father's side, I have one living relative but she had dementia, so it isn't like she knows who I am anymore."

"I'm sorry," Grayson said. "That must be hard."

"It's been that way for so long now that I rarely ever think about what my grandmother used to be like when I was a teenager," she said. "Besides, I was away at boarding school for much of the year anyway. When I was home, I had other priorities like Zoya and my cousin Charlie. I didn't make time for her and then it was suddenly too late.

Her mind was gone." She exhaled and her shoulders slumped. Since Ms. Primm, her etiquette teacher, would have a heart attack if she saw Kyra right now, she forced her shoulders back and sat up straighter. Another sip of coffee helped wake her up.

"Isn't it funny how easy it is to take everyone for granted?" Grayson asked, but the question was obviously rhetorical. "It's so easy to fall into the trap of thinking everyone will wake up each day and nothing major will change." He snapped his fingers. "Then, just like that everything you believed you know can be stripped from you."

Kyra nodded. "You suddenly realize the whole world doesn't revolve around you and, in fact, stops for those we care about."

"I always wanted to take the Marshall out for a cold beer and clear the air," Grayson said.

Ian nodded. "This might sound strange but I've been feeling the exact same way."

"Even if he rejected me and said he couldn't stand me, I could at least clear the air. There was so much left unsaid," Grayson said with a small nod toward his brother.

"Exactly. He wasn't an easy person to be around and I couldn't relate to him on any level other than loving Texas and the family ranch," Ian said.

"Same here," Grayson agreed.

Kyra saw the remorse in both men's eyes and hoped she hadn't stirred up emotions that were too painful for them.

"Since we can't go back and change the past, we might as well focus on the future instead." Grayson pointed toward the iPad. "We're less than twenty-four hours from the meet-up spot. Time to come up with a plan."

Ian rolled the table in between him and where Kyra was sitting. Since the only other place to sit was the bed, Grayson took the spot next to her and tried not to focus on how sitting next to her, *being* with her, felt like the most natural thing. Ian set the iPad on top of the table and pulled up the downtown area with Reunion Tower that sat on Reunion Blvd. Stemmons Freeway was a stone's toss away and S. Houston Street sat behind the tall tower and observation deck. There was an Amtrak station at the corner of S. Houston and Reunion Blvd. A train station split the difference. The tower was beside Hyatt Regency. There was so much going on in the downtown area and too many places a sniper could hide. They would be vulnerable and exposed at the Tower, and that didn't sit well with Grayson.

"Where are you supposed to meet and at what time?" Ian asked.

"The bar in the restaurant at the top of Reunion Tower," Kyra supplied.

Ian's gaze widened as he studied the map.

"There are so many vulnerable places in this area," Grayson said.

"I was just thinking the same thing," Ian said. "It's next to impossible to cover every single angle." He pointed to the top of the Courtyard by Marriott across the street. "A sniper could be here." He pointed to the La Quinta beside that. "Or here."

"There are so many rooftops, not to mention open parking beside the building," Grayson stated.

"Doesn't leave us a whole lot of options," Ian said.

"They'll be looking for her, and possibly Zoya too, unless they have someone watching her house," Grayson reasoned.

Kyra nodded. "It's a safe bet."

"My security will keep watch over her. She'll be fine," Grayson reassured when Kyra chewed on her bottom lip. She nodded again but her concern was obvious in the way she fidgeted. One moment, she tucked her hair behind her ear. The next, she was working the hem of her shirt between her fingers. The wheels were turning as she studied the map, her eyes searching for an angle.

"What if we go underground?" she asked.

"They'll have folks there," Ian stated. "It's the first thing we would think of, so they'll have that covered."

Grayson figured his brother was onto something. He grabbed his cell phone and looked up events at Reunion Arena. Hit the jackpot when he saw that a band would be playing next weekend.

"We can walk right through the front doors of the hotel," Grayson said, a plan hatching in his mind. He locked gazes with his brother as Kyra fidgeted on the bed, causing her outer thigh to graze his. He was getting used to the jolt of electricity that came with contact to the point of wanting it.

Ian's smile was ear-to-ear. "We know a thing or two about having someone famous in the family."

"All we need is one of those fancy RVs," Grayson said. "Something big and sleek. Something in a shiny black. Bands never put their name on the RV that contains the star, so we'll fit right in with something that looks expensive."

"What are the two of you talking about?" Kyra's gaze bounced from Ian's back to Grayson's. "And why don't stars have their names on the sides of their RV? Wouldn't they want the free advertising?

"This is Texas. No one will be surprised to see a country and western tour bus docking downtown," Grayson explained. "Reunion Arena is next door. And stars put their names on the equipment bus that follows them usually by a few hours. The reason stars travel in an unmarked RV is for privacy's sake. At least that's the way Raleigh Perry travels now that her career has national attention."

"Hold on a second." Kyra's eyes widened and her jaw nearly hit the bed. "Are you saying that you know Raleigh Perry?"

"Wait...are you saying you *do*?" Grayson asked.

"Everybody knows her music," Kyra stated like it was as obvious as the nose on her face. "*The Loft* is probably the best song I've ever heard."

"Then you should come by the ranch sometime," Ian interjected.

"No." Kyra shook her head. Then, she seemed to realize they weren't kidding. "You're serious, aren't you?"

"Raleigh Perry is our newly minted sister-in-law," Ian explained.

Kyra smacked the table with the flat of her palm. "Get out. You two are playing a trick on me!" She studied Ian and then Grayson. "Nope. You're telling the truth. I can see it in your eyes."

Grayson put his hands in the air, palms up, in the surrender position. "You got me."

"Our mother used to babysit her when she was all red hair and freckles," Ian said.

"That's so amazing," Kyra said. It was funny to see a royal fangirl gush over Raleigh. It was also endearing to see Kyra's expression.

"*The Loft* was written in our barn," Grayson said, enjoying seeing Kyra's eyes light up when they talked about his sister-in-law. Raleigh was a sweet person and she deserved all her success. "When she got into trouble on tour with a bomb threat that turned out to be very real, she came back to Lone Star Pass and reconnected with our brother Brax."

"That's incredible," Kyra said with a sense of awe in her voice. She reached over and planted a hand on Grayson's thigh. "Do you think I could meet her?"

Grayson laughed.

"That can be arranged," he said. "But first, let's get you to your meet-up."

"Agreed," she said before adding, "alive."

11

Kyra studied the map, leaving her hand on Grayson's thigh. There was something about physically connecting with him that kept her nerves a level below panic. The electricity pinging between them couldn't be ignored but there was also a sense of comfort that was difficult to understand, let alone explain when they touched.

"Won't it be obvious that I'm not a country and western star?" Kyra asked.

"That's the beauty in the plan," Grayson stated. His eyes sparked when he had an idea and they were even more beautiful if that was possible. She had no idea how he planned to pull off slipping her into the hotel and then over to the Tower without being recognized. Whoever was after her would have a very strong idea of who she was and what she looked like. Appearances could be changed but only so much.

"How so?" she asked.

"The more negative attention we create, the more people will look away instead of toward," Grayson said. She must have made quite the face because his hand almost immediately shot up. "You just have to appear obnoxiously drunk to sell the notion."

"Won't more people look at me that way?" She really was confused.

"People, yes. The people looking for you...no," he explained.

"How do you plan to pull this off?" she asked.

"Obviously, your appearance will have to be changed," Grayson started.

"I'm envisioning ripped jeans shorts with cowgirl boots," Ian took over as Grayson nodded. "Some type of blouse that will be unbuttoned a little too low."

Grayson's muscles tensed at the mention of the last part but he grudgingly nodded.

"Your hair will have to be in braids to disguise all the curls," Ian continued. "And, of course, you'll be wearing a cowgirl hat so it'll be more difficult for your face to be seen."

A picture was emerging and Kyra was beginning to understand.

"We can probably drum up an acoustic guitar considering we're in a major city," Ian continued. "I'll pick up a bottle of vodka from the liquor store before we head over."

"Can you have all this arranged so quickly?" she asked, thinking this was a pretty major feat.

"Throw enough money around, and you'd be surprised at everything you can get done," Ian said.

"We have a saying in America...*money talks*," Ian stated.

"Money does seem to be at the root of a whole lot of problems," Grayson said, "but it solves some of them too."

"It sure seems to be the root of the evil my father is dealing with," Kyra said, feeling nothing but disdain for her father's enemies or anyone who would use her country to hide criminal activity. She couldn't help but feel frustrated at how money changed people and how greed turned them into monsters.

"Not everyone who has money cares about more than putting food on the table," Grayson said, and his tone was all no-nonsense.

"And not everyone abuses their wealth," Ian added as his brother nodded.

She'd probably just spoken a little too harshly but it was frustrating how some people could turn something that should be nothing but good into a quest to take more and destroy everything and everyone in their way.

"More people should be like you and your brother," she said to Ian. "The world would be a better place."

Ian smirked. "You aren't going to get any arguments out of me there."

Grayson was already busy on his phone, no doubt pulling together supplies and figuring out how to rent an RV. She glanced over at his cell and confirmed what she was thinking.

"How do you plan to get everything here in time?" she asked.

"You'd be surprised at what you can accomplish with enough money," he stated without looking up from his phone.

Maybe she should be, but this experience would scar the way she viewed money for the rest of her life. She could see why Grayson and his brother chose to focus on working the land and raising cattle than worry about how many zeroes they had in their bank accounts. Based on the fact they ran the largest cattle operation in Texas, the numbers had to be significant. They also seemed able to get pretty much anything they wanted on a moment's notice. Kyra's country itself wasn't the wealthiest in Europe. Her father did all right and she'd grown up with enough privilege to know it. Her father had moved among the people without conveying an image of being above them. In fact, he cared so much about his people that he probably worried too much. His heart condition was most likely the result of the stress that came with running a country alone.

"Bingo," Grayson said, clearly proud of himself for doing something. "I got an RV. It's big and sleek, and should help sell the cover story."

He held up his screen, tilting it so both her and Ian could see.

"Looks nice," Ian said with more than a hint of pride in his voice. "Way to go, big brother."

"Wow," was all Kyra could say. "And this can be delivered in time?"

"The owner is bringing it over right now," Grayson said. "There's an app for pretty much anything right now. I found this on RV Share. A business would have been more difficult to secure at this time of night so I went with a personal approach."

"You really got that from an app?" Ian sounded even more impressed.

"Figured it would be the best approach under the circumstances," Grayson admitted.

"Way to go," Ian said. The love between brothers was so easy to read and it made Kyra wish she'd grown up with siblings. At least she'd had Charlie. *Charlie.* She could only hope he was okay. The thought of losing him after everything they'd been through together was more than she could handle. It would be all too easy to slip into the sinkhole of worry under the circumstances, which wouldn't do anyone any good. In times like these, staying positive was the only approach because doing anything else would only drag her spirits down. She couldn't allow herself to go to that place where something bad had happened to her father or Charlie. Thinking otherwise without proof was too depressing. She admired people who could go through times like these and hold it together, stay positive. With her, it required effort on her part not to slide down a negative slope.

She gave herself bonus points for dragging herself out of the pit of despair. Some days were easier than others. Having help made a huge difference. As much as Kyra loved Zoya, she wasn't equipped to deal with this kind of stressful situation. Her friend had a normal life. She'd gone to university in America and then graduate school. Her parents did well, but not so well anyone would target them or their daughter. Zoya hadn't grown up taking self-defense classes. And as much as Kyra had loved practicing martial arts, she also had a feeling the skills might come in handy someday. Growing up in a palace, she'd been confronted with overzealous subjects a couple times. Someone who protested on the lawn or had to be subdued because they climbed through a window to get closer to the king. She'd been sheltered from much of what happened when she was younger. As she grew older and roamed more freely around the palace, she'd had a few encounters that had left her shaken...and then determined.

GRAYSON GLANCED over at Kyra when she'd been quiet a little too long. Her top teeth scraped across her bottom lip, a sure sign she was deep in thought. He nudged her gently with his elbow.

"Everything okay?" he asked. Then said, "Hold on. Stupid question. Tell me what you're thinking."

She shrugged. "I'm trying not to think about my father's safety or my cousin's. I'm trying not to let my imagination run away with me, because it can in times of stress. I'm trying not to get too deep inside my head while we're coming up with our game plan."

Grayson set his phone down on the bed and wrapped an arm around her shoulders. "Is it okay if I do this?"

She leaned into him and nodded as Ian excused himself, mumbling something about heading out to pick up food.

"Would it make you feel any better if I told you how incredibly brave I think you are?" Grayson asked as the door closed behind Ian.

"Surprisingly...yes," she admitted. Then, she looked up with blue eyes glittery with something that looked a whole lot like need.

All Grayson wanted to do in this moment was make her feel safe, preferably in his arms. He ached to look after her, care for her, and give her one moment in this day that wasn't just about survival. More than anything, he wanted to feel her lips moving against his.

Since he didn't want to misinterpret her signals, he said, "I'd very much like to kiss you."

She didn't answer with words. Instead, she tilted her mouth toward his and kissed him. The kiss was soft at first but quickly morphed into a tangle of tongues and labored breaths. Grayson couldn't decide whether he should lean into the moment or back away so both of them could get some perspective before the situation got out of control. *Lean in,* he decided, bringing his hand up to cup her face and position her mouth for better access. When she bit his bottom lip and tugged at it between her teeth, other parts of his body woke up. Parts that might make it awkward should his brother walk inside the room anytime soon.

So, with all the effort he could muster, he pulled back. Kyra exhaled and her disappointment nearly caused him to say *what the hell* and go for what they both wanted.

What they both needed.

But walking in on the two of them having sex would most likely traumatize Ian for many years to come. Plus, sex wasn't exactly on the table as an option, despite the fact neither seemed able to regulate their breathing after those steamy kisses.

"It was probably a good idea to stop," Kyra said without much conviction in her words.

"It was a terrible idea if you ask me, but necessary," he quickly countered. "Besides, it's probably just the heat of the moment that has you wanting...*this*."

"There was plenty of heat in the moment but that's not the reason..."

She stopped herself midsentence. The rosy hue returned to her cheeks and he chided himself for embarrassing her.

"We got out of hand for a second but we're thinking clearly again," he continued, trying to give her an out so it didn't become awkward between them.

Kyra's shoulders deflated as she exhaled, long and slow. "I hear what you're saying but I'm perfectly capable of determining whether or not I'm running on heightened emotions or not. You don't have to kiss me again. That's entirely up to you. But I won't take it back or regret what was by far the best kiss of my entire life. Even if that sounds a little silly to someone with your experience."

She folded her arms across her chest like she was creating a barrier for incoming pain as Grayson considered her words.

"I asked permission to kiss you a minute ago and I have every intention of asking again when the time is right," he started. "I've never had a kiss get out-of-hand on me like that one just did. But then I've never met anyone like you before. So, I'm likely to stumble my way through this...whatever *this* is that's happening between us. It's real on my side and I'm hoping like hell it's real on yours as well."

"No need to hope. I've never been this attracted to someone before," she admitted and the blush returned to her cheeks.

Grayson brought his hand up to her face and used the pad of his thumb to trace her jawline. "You're beautiful. Inside and out. You're strong. But you're also like no one I've ever met before and I'm playing catch up as to what that means to me."

Kyra locked gazes with him for a few seconds before she pushed up to standing. "Yeah? I hope you figure it out soon, because no one knows how much time they have left and it'd be a shame to waste this moment."

It was probably for the best she left the room after that because he'd just messed up big time. The whole attraction caught him off guard. Logic said this whole ordeal would be over soon enough and the two of them would go about their lives in different countries. He lived on a ranch with very little cell coverage and preferred it that way. Talk about a long-distance fling. Plus, everyone knew they never lasted.

He heard the shower turn on and had to talk himself out of knocking on the door. Their conversation was left unfinished and now he'd put them in a position that was awkward as hell. Were they into each other? The chemistry between them was off the charts of anything he'd ever felt before. Some of it had to do with the fact they'd almost died. He wasn't naïve enough to sweep that under the rug. It was serious, driven by biology. They'd almost died. They needed proof of life.

There wasn't much more life affirming than making love.

A voice in the back of his mind pointed out his attraction to Kyra was so much more than chemistry. Her mind was sharp. She was clearly intelligent and a quick thinker. Those were traits he admired in the opposite sex. Physical appearance only went so far if there was nothing to back it up. The prettiest person changed in his eyes quickly once they started talking. The attraction either grew or fizzled. Far too many times, it was the latter. With Kyra, it was taking on a life of its own.

Practically speaking, theirs would be a short-lived fling if it got off the ground. This whole scenario could be over in less than twenty-four hours. Then what?

Grayson needed to remind himself of the temporary nature of their relationship as many times as necessary to keep this in perspective. With Kyra, it would be a little too easy to let things get out of hand and for an attraction to run wild.

Darn shame, he decided. Because she was truly unlike anyone he'd ever met before.

The spigot cut off. A few seconds later, a towel-wrapped princess exited the bathroom. Her hair fell in damp ringlets and beads of water trickled down her shoulders and into the V of her chest. Grayson forced his gaze away from those lucky water drops while trying to keep a handle on his attraction. Kyra was intelligent and beautiful. She had a body made for sinning on Sunday, and all Grayson could focus on was one of those droplets as it rolled across creamy skin and disappeared between full breasts.

12

"Excuse me. Do you mind turning your head the other way?" Kyra had been so flustered when she'd stalked off to the bathroom a little while ago, she'd forgotten to bring fresh clothes. There she stood, naked as the day was long, with only a towel protecting her modesty, praying Ian didn't pick this moment to walk through the door.

Grayson complied with her request, turning his head toward the curtains as Kyra scooped up the bag with clothes.

"You can turn back now," she said after sprinting to the bathroom. Part of her wanted to sit down and talk about what had just happened between them but it was a one-time runaway train. What was there to discuss? She needed to not get kidnapped or killed while her father found an ally country willing to go up against one of the most dangerous organized crime rings in Europe.

In the meantime, she also needed to not fall for the guy helping her stay away from kidnappers and would-be killers. It sounded simple enough. Stay alive. Keep an emotional distance from Grayson. But the man in the room stirred so many feelings in her chest—feelings she'd never experienced to this degree with anyone before him. It was confusing and somehow not. Confusing in the sense that she had no idea what it would mean in a relationship and not because these feelings also felt like the most natural thing with Grayson.

Distracting herself, she refocused on something that made more sense. Charlie. If only there was a way to get a message to her cousin. She still had no idea if he was alive. There'd be no use kidnapping him. Her father would only abdicate for her. She was his weak link even though he cared for Charlie very much. Besides, Charlie would never expect the king to hand over the keys to his kingdom. Charlie loved Serentia as much as her father. Kyra, on the other hand, loved the people but nothing else about being a royal. Born into duty, there wasn't much choice in the matter.

With a deep sigh, she dressed in fresh clothing and checked herself in the mirror. There'd be no pajamas tonight. She would spend the next hour preparing. The idea of her pulling off looking like a country and western star almost made her laugh. Could she fool anyone trying to find her?

Rummaging around in the bag, she located a pair of pajama bottoms. There was a ribbon used as a drawstring. She pulled it out of the pants and managed to rip it in half. While her hair was still wet, she parted it down the middle and then styled it in twin fishtail braids. She tied off the ends with the ribbon. After examining herself in the mirror, she decided she wasn't off to a bad start. This look went a long way toward selling the country and western star. With a cowgirl hat, she might be able to cover enough of her face to get away with walking right past a would-be kidnapper. She would refer to the person pursuing her as *this* instead of murderer. If someone had wanted her dead, they would have shot her from a distance earlier.

Thinking back to the man at the condo, he hadn't had a weapon at the ready. Had he planned on overpowering her physically? If he'd intended to kill her, wouldn't he have had a weapon in hand when he reached the door?

She wished she could go back and force him to talk. Logic said he wouldn't, so she didn't spend any more energy going down the road of wishful thinking. Staying rooted in reality could mean the difference between life and death.

By the time she returned to the main area, Ian was back. His arms were loaded down with bags.

"I think I found everything we need," he said as he glanced up at her. He momentarily froze. "Wow. Those braids definitely work for the look we're going for."

Grayson gave a curt nod before taking several of the bags from his brother. "What else do you have in here?"

"Shorts and boots like we talked about." Ian set the other bags down on the table along with a pair of pizza boxes.

"Do you mind if I eat?" Kyra asked, the smell practically causing her mouth to water.

"Go for it," Ian said. "There should be napkins and maybe some plates in that bag." He pointed to the white bag with red lettering, *Ang and Vito's*.

"What about you guys? Are you going to eat?" she asked as they dumped bags on the second bed.

"Be right there," Ian said while Grayson nodded.

From all appearances, Grayson had gone inside himself. He seemed caught off guard after her reaction a few minutes ago. She had to keep her head in the game, so she wrote off his tense expression. At the moment, her own safety trumped every other thought.

"I'll make plates." She figured it was the least she could do after the two brothers had served all of her meals and brought her coffee, not that she minded the last part. Kyra busied herself filling plates and setting out napkins. When she was finished, she glanced over at the bed. Her gaze stopped on a packet. "What's that?"

Ian's gaze followed her finger where she pointed.

"Oh, those are temporary tattoos. I figure the more 'ink' we put on you and the more belligerent you are when we arrive at the hotel, the better. People generally think it's rude to stare, even when you give them a reason," he stated.

Kyra nodded. "I'm used to getting attention everywhere I go in my country, but intentionally drawing negative attention will be new for me."

"You'll do great," Ian said. Grayson was still busy, keeping quiet. She liked it better when he was talking. With his solemn expression, she didn't have a clue what he was thinking.

"Food's ready." She picked up a plate and perched on the opposite bed. A pizza slice covered her entire plate. The crust was perfectly cooked. The cheese warm and just gooey enough. "Where did you find this place?"

"It was highly rated on one of those food apps," Ian said. "Is it good?"

"Good is not nearly a good enough word for this taste," she said.

Ian took the couple of steps over to the table with Grayson right behind. Both grabbed a plate and got busy. No one said a word until the one box was empty and the other one had two slices left.

"Anyone want this?" Ian asked, motioning toward the last two.

"I'm stuffed. I couldn't eat another bite if I tried," Kyra admitted.

"Knock yourself out," Grayson said. At least he was doing more than nodding when it came to his brother.

Ian finished off the last of the pizza while she straightened the place up.

"No offense, but don't you have servants who do this for you where you live?" Ian asked. She must've shot him quite the look because he immediately threw his hands up in the air, palms out in the surrender position. "I hope you don't take offense."

"Don't worry. I won't." The comment stung a little bit, though. Mainly because it was true. "When I'm home there are people who attend to me. While I was in college, I insisted on living in a dorm and living just like every other college student."

"How'd that work out for you?" Ian asked.

Kyra laughed. "I was pretty much the only student who never had to use the emergency phone while walking around campus late at night."

"I can't imagine living under that kind of scrutiny," Ian admitted. "We live in a fishbowl back home to a certain extent. But nothing like what you must have gone through."

"Honestly, I was so used to it, that having security occupy the dorm room next to me felt like freedom," she said.

"How about now?" Ian asked.

"I've never felt more trapped and freer all at once," she said without hesitation. Truths had a way of coming out when the filter was disengaged and she spoke without thinking, without talking herself out of her real truth. Then again, she'd been trained what to say, when to speak, and how to say everything. "Duty requires me to act a certain way when I'm home."

"Have you ever thought about not going back?" Ian's forehead crunched up with the question, but it was Grayson's interest in her answer that caught her eye. His gaze flew to her despite keeping his head down so she could barely see his eyes.

"Yes. When I was in college, I contemplated asking to stay in Canada to get a job," she admitted.

"Why didn't you?" Ian continued, throwing his empty plate in the bag she'd set out for trash.

"I didn't want to disappoint my father, I guess," she said, and that was partially true. She'd also been too scared to go to him and make the request. What if he'd said yes? Where would she be then? Living in Canada with a job? "At twenty-two, I didn't know what I wanted. So, I went home after I graduated and stepped into my role as princess."

"What about now?" Grayson suddenly perked up. "Do you know what you want now?"

"WHAT I WANT NOW IS IRRELEVANT," Kyra said before closing up the trash bag and then placing it outside the door.

Grayson went back to work on the plan for tomorrow night, shoving his other personal questions for the princess aside. She joined them, picking through the temporary tattoos.

"How about this rope around my arm?" she asked.

"That would work," Grayson said. He picked up one that said *cowgirl up* in cursive before staring at her left wrist. "May I?"

She lifted her hand but not her gaze. "Go ahead."

He took hold of her wrist, realizing how small it was by comparison and how soft her skin was against the roughness of his fingers. He placed the temporary tattoo running longways on her delicate wrist. He nearly cracked a smile thinking how deadly one flick could be if she was holding a metal star.

"That would look nice there," she said, clearing her throat. She slicked her tongue across her bottom lip, leaving a silky trail. *Dangerous,* he thought.

"I've seen them on others and thought it would help you fit in." Grayson could hear the huskiness in his own voice.

"It'll help with the image," she said, looking like she was being careful not to make eye contact when they were this close. She brought her free hand up and covered her wrist tattoo placement with it.

"I was also thinking this one..." He picked up a bucking bronco tattoo. "Might go nicely here." He took a knee before placing the temporary tattoo on the outside of her right thigh.

"I could see that," she said. She took it from him and wrapped it around her arm. "Or maybe here."

Ian ripped the sleeves off of a flannel shirt. "Either of those would work. We'll need an arm tattoo so we can show it off."

"Which one do you like better? The rope or the bronco?" Grayson asked.

"Maybe the rope around my arm and the bronco on my thigh," she stated after a thoughtful pause.

"We might as well test them out and see how it looks," Ian said. "They'll hold for a couple of days so we should be fine."

"Okay," Kyra said. "Where should we start?"

"The thigh," Grayson said as Ian immediately excused himself and left the room. "Then, I can work my way up." He heard how that sounded but addressing the comment would only draw more attention to it.

Kyra handed over the bronco. He read the directions for the ink transfer before handing them back to Kyra.

"This is basically what we did as kids, but better quality," she said after reading the instructions.

Grayson nodded. "Are you ready?"

She inhaled a deep breath. "Ready as I'll ever be."

He went to work on the transfer. The rope came out remarkably well. "It needs to dry for twenty minutes or so."

"I'll be careful," she promised.

"What do you think about this one?" He motioned toward one he'd set aside.

"A dragonfly? It's beautiful, but what does it symbolize?" she asked.

"It means different things depending on the culture. For me, it symbolizes strength and courage through change. Freedom," he said.

"I like that a lot actually," she responded.

"I'd like to place this one right here." He lifted his finger to her right hip near the waistband of her pants. "Is it okay to touch you?"

"Yes," she said a little breathlessly as she lifted her shirt and exposed bare skin.

Grayson pressed the temporary tattoo against her body, flattening it by spreading his fingers. Kyra sucked in a breath, compressed her lips, and shifted her gaze to the curtain wall on the opposite side of the room.

Slowly, she released the breath she'd been holding. As he looked up at her, he could see her pulse pounding at the base of her throat. The air in the room charged with electricity, causing every one of his muscles to cord with tension. Grayson gripped both sides of Kyra's waist. For a long moment, neither spoke.

"I think we've found enough, don't you?" she asked. And then she took a step back.

"These should work nicely," he agreed, pushing off the bed to standing, trying to find an outlet for the frissons of heat coursing through his body.

"Okay then, looks like I have a whole getup here," she continued, surveying the bed, not making eye contact. Could she? Or did it feel like doing so would push them both past the point of no return?

Grayson moved to his phone that was now buzzing, grateful for the distraction. He checked the screen and realized he'd missed a text from the RV owner. "Looks like your ride is on its way."

"Good," she said after clearing her throat. "I should probably memorize the layout of the hotel and start locating escape points."

Grayson nodded.

"When will the RV arrive?" she asked, her tone all business now.

"It's coming in from the Austin area so three to four hours depending on traffic," he said, moving over to the iPad. He entered the password and then handed it over to Kyra. He checked the time. "At this hour, I would expect a smooth drive."

Which was the opposite of how he felt about navigating his relationship with Kyra because his heart recognized how different she was from everyone he'd met before but logic warned not to go down that road.

13

Kyra studied the layout of Reunion Tower. She studied the layout of the Hyatt. She studied the roads around the area, taking note of the direction of one-way streets as they led to and from the hotel. Knowledge was powerful.

"Do you, by chance, have pictures of the RV?" she asked Grayson as Ian joined them from the bathroom.

"Right here," Grayson said, moving next to her. He tapped the screen a couple of times and then images populated the screen. "There's a 3D tour as well."

"Good. Thanks," she said without looking up. It was bad enough she was breathing in his spicy male scent. She didn't need to go there with looking into those blue eyes.

"Did you get all the tattoos worked out?" Ian asked, his gaze slowly taking in his brother and then her. He must be as confused about the nature of their relationship as she was. Correction, *used* to be. Now, she was crystal clear that, despite their intense attraction, a real relationship wasn't a possibility. Neither one had to spell out the fact he was a rancher and she was a princess. It was obvious their lives wouldn't allow for anything more than casual contact and the chemistry between them would want more. No use touching a hot stove when nothing could be done to change it.

"Yes," they both said in unison.

Ian compressed his lips like he was stopping himself from speaking his mind. Then, he smiled and threw his dirty clothes in a bag inside his duffel.

"What's the status?" Ian took a seat on the edge of the second bed.

"RV is on its way," Grayson said. "We'll have it in plenty of time to get acquainted with every inch. In the meantime, Kyra is memorizing layouts."

"We'll each need to do the same," Ian said.

Grayson nodded.

"I'll leave you guys to the iPad while I go in the bathroom and tattoo myself," Kyra said, needing to put a little space in between her and Grayson. There was only so much electricity a person could take. She gathered up the artwork they'd settled on and headed to the bathroom so she could be alone. She wished she could use the iPad or a phone to make contact with Charlie but the risks were too great. Plus, she would see him in a matter of hours. The clock was winding down on the meetup. He would be there. She wouldn't allow herself to consider any other option.

After carefully studying the maps, she questioned the decision to meet up at Reunion Tower. There might be multiple elevators but meeting at the bar made it difficult to escape. Once up at the bar, there weren't many ways down, potentially stranding her.

Having Grayson and Ian there would be the difference between taking a stupid risk and playing it smart. She could describe her cousin, possibly give them a decent sketch.

Although, art class in college had been years ago and she hadn't kept up her skills.

Maybe she could search for an actor who Charlie resembled. One immediately came to mind. The redhead who played Harry Potter's best friend in the movies. Ron Weasley. Now that she had a good visual to give the others, she meticulously applied each tattoo. The one on her hip caused a trill of awareness to skitter through her at the memory of Grayson's hands on her. Hands that were rough from working outside.

Kyra shook off the thought, clearing her mind of Grayson and his hands.

When the last tattoo had been applied, she checked herself in the mirror. Between the braids and the tattoos, a transformation was definitely happening. Good. She was starting to believe they might actually pull off tricking others when she added a hat and all different clothing. There was no hiding her fair skin, though. That might prove tricky.

She exited the bathroom and joined the others who were huddled over the table, studying the iPad. They both glanced up around the same time.

"Wow," Ian said.

Grayson was quiet but his eyes widened and she took it as a good sign that she was making the transformation they all hoped for.

"My only concern is how fair-skinned I am. Isn't that a dead giveaway?" she asked.

"Hold on." Ian moved around the table to the bed. He shifted around the bags until he found a can. He held it up. "Self-tanner should help with that."

Kyra crossed the room and took the offering. She examined the spray can. "I'll be right back."

In the bathroom, she slipped out of her outfit and into the shower. After reading the instructions, she went to town spraying every inch of her legs, body, and arms. She carefully sprayed her neck before spraying one of her hands and then applying it to her face. The result was remarkable. At this rate, there was no need to change the color of her hair. The transformation between the tan and the tattoos was astounding. Add the clothes and an RV, and voila! Her confidence in the plan was building. Grayson and Ian made sense as bodyguards or roadies. Probably bodyguards considering the sheer amount of muscles on both.

This could actually work. She might be able to pull this off after all.

When she returned from the bathroom this time after dressing, Grayson was sketching something out on a piece of paper while Ian looked on intently. He pointed at it and they both spoke in hushed tones, no doubt coming up with possible entry points and escape routes as she had earlier. She trusted their judgment and was trusting them with her life.

Yet, it was still important for her to come up with her own plan in the event she was separated from them. She'd learned a long time ago not to rely on others for her safety. Once a criminal snuck into the palace and managed to get into her bedroom suite in the timeframe her devoted nanny happened to be downstairs making a midnight snack. Kyra had screamed and fought him off long enough for help to arrive but if no one had been within earshot, the creep would have kidnapped her.

In that moment, she'd made a promise never to be vulnerable again. Her caregivers were well-intentioned, but no one could be around twenty-four-seven. Kyra had been ten years old. The next morning she brought it up with her father and he'd suggested she start taking martial ats classes with her cousin.

"How did I do?" She twirled.

"You look like a different person," Ian said, more than a hint of pride in his voice.

"I like the other version better, but this is convincing and that's what we need right now," Grayson said. His brother shot him a look of disapproval at the comment, But Kyra understood the meaning and took it as the compliment he meant.

She smiled at him.

"Since neither of you have met my cousin Charlie, I thought I might give you an idea of what he looked like. Did either of you watch any of the Harry Potter movies?" she asked.

Both shook their heads.

"Seriously?" Even though she'd had a protected life and everything about her existence had been perfectly curated, she'd watched the movies. Granted, she'd watched them in college but still.

"Nope." Ian shook his head.

"I read the first book," Grayson said. "It was good."

"Okay, fine. Google the first movie and I'll show you who my cousin looks like," she said.

They did.

Kyra walked over and pulled up a picture of Ron Weasley. "That's him. That's my Charlie."

"Being a royal, wouldn't it be easy to Google a picture of him?" Ian asked.

"He's not technically a royal. He's from my mother's side of the family, not my father's. Charlie has been kept away from all that exposure on purpose," she explained. "Being a small country, we've been able to protect his privacy and he has never wanted a public life."

Each brother grabbed their cell phones and snapped a picture.

"All right," Ian said.

The sun was already coming up and the clock was ticking. Roughly thirteen hours to the meetup, give or take. All the preparation was coming together, and Kyra could think of a half dozen scenarios where everything blew up in their faces.

Grayson's phone buzzed while still in his hand. "Looks like the RV has arrived."

GRAYSON EXCUSED HIMSELF. He met a guy by the name of Bud in front of the hotel as the sun was rising. It was a beautiful Texas morning and, he hoped, a good omen for the day. Bud stood around six feet tall and had a beer belly that was barely contained in his button-down shirt. He wore a belt buckle half the size of Texas, jeans, and boots. His Stetson hooded his face as he walked over, keys in hand.

"She's filled up with gas and has a couple days' worth of water and food inside, like you requested," Bud said. The two shook hands. Bud had a firm grip, the hallmark of an honest person. Close up, he had a round face and a kind smile. "She's ready to go."

"Much appreciated," Grayson said. He pulled out his cell and made a fund transfer.

Bud fished out his cell after handing over the keys.

"That's twice the amount advertised," Bud said, eyes wide.

"I threw in a short-notice, fast-delivery bonus," Grayson said.

"Thank you, sir." Bud studied Grayson for a long moment. "You sure do look familiar."

"I get that a lot," Grayson said.

"Where do I know you from?" Bud continued. "Rodeo?"

"Nah, not me."

"I know. The movies. You were in that one with..." Bud snapped his fingers.

"You got me," Grayson said.

"Mind if I get a picture for the wife?" Bud asked.

"Would it be all right if we did it when I return the RV, instead of now?" Grayson had no idea if Bud's wife would recognize him and place him, but he wanted to hold off for now. He didn't need his face showing up on social media right before he was about to put his life on the line. Not that Bud's life would crossover with the criminals targeting Kyra but the guy from the condo would be able to ID Grayson. He had no idea if the guy was out of jail yet.

"Sure," Bud said with a hint of disappointment in his voice.

"We'll make sure they're good ones," Grayson said.

"All right. I gotcha." It seemed to dawn on Bud that Grayson might want to maintain a sense of privacy. "Later is fine."

"Thank you," Grayson said, and he meant it.

"Do you need a walk-thru on the RV?" Bud asked.

"All I need are these." Grayson held up the set of keys. "The rest I can figure out for myself."

"I'll just be a few minutes more. All I need to do is unhook my Jeep so I can make the drive home," Bud said.

"Take your time." Grayson was in no hurry and this would give him a chance to get familiar with the RV anyway.

Bud would be nearby in the event a question came up. Plus, the meetup wasn't for a little more than twelve hours. Being out of the hotel room and away from Kyra wasn't the worst thing for Grayson. He was having a difficult time keeping his feelings in perspective with her in the room and couldn't afford a distraction. "I'll just check her out from the inside."

Bud smiled and saluted. The guy seemed like a sweetheart. Big teddy bear type.

Grayson took note of the doors and exits, mainly three. There was a door on the driver's side, the passenger side, and one on the right side of the RV. This was a custom job but the basic layout was the same. The finishes were high end and there was a flat-screen TV on a wall that extended out once the RV was parked. Grayson didn't plan on needing to use that feature. He'd rented the RV for a week, the minimum requirement, but didn't plan to need it beyond tonight. He could return it early by asking Bud to pick it up or arranging a driver to take it back to Austin for Grayson. Either way.

Inside, the driver and passenger seats were basically Lazy-Boys. Those might come in handy after the meetup. Speaking of which, they'd done a whole lot of planning for that moment but what happened after? Kyra had been separated from Charlie and the security team once already. Grayson needed to have a conversation with her about her next steps beyond the Tower, because the threat wasn't going away when she was reunited with her team. Grayson could offer assistance with planning the next move. He also wanted to figure out how her location had been pinpointed at the condo, where the leak came from. He had his suspicions but that was all. There was no confirmation he'd been on the right track with the cell phone tracking software. Speaking of which, no news from his security team with

Zoya was probably good news. Still, he texted them requesting an update.

The way he understood the cell phone software was that once someone hacked into a phone, all the person's contacts could be hacked as well. But what if Charlie's phone had been hacked or Pietro's? There was a third guy...Marko. What about one of their phones?

Bud went to work unhitching the Jeep. He was done before Grayson made it to the back of the RV. Then again, Bud did this either for a living or on the side. It seemed like everyone Grayson knew had a side business these days in addition to working a regular job or tending shop for a store owner in Lone Star Pass. Everyone was looking for a way to keep up and earn a living. He respected the hell out of folks for their hustle. It always humbled him and reminded him of just how much he'd been given being born a Firebrand. A guaranteed job, roof over his head, food on the table. He didn't take any of those things for granted.

The RV had granite countertops, a full-size stainless-steel fridge that was stocked with drinks and ready to heat meals. Six people could survive here for days without making a pitstop, which was exactly the idea. This was the backup plan if everything went south. He'd have this baby parked in the lot behind the Hyatt in the open lot. They could load up and hit the highway in a matter of minutes should the need arise. The Hyatt had a back exit that wound through the grand ballrooms and down a hallway.

The lot was perfect. It was large enough to accommodate the oversized vehicle. Grayson walked the RV, memorizing the layout as he checked cabinets and searched for hiding spots.

The impressive RV had hydraulic slide-outs on both sides and a living room that might be as large as Grayson's cabin back home on the ranch. The gray granite counter-tops and tile backsplash were higher-end than the materials in Grayson's home. His taste was clean and simple. According to an information sheet that had been placed on the table, this thing had heated porcelain tile floors. Those probably came in handy for some states, but Texas didn't need 'em. The rest of the furniture was some high-end leather job. In back was a king-sized bed and a 40-inch 4K LED television. The one in the living room was 50-inch and, apparently, with a few button pushes the room could turn into a movie theatre setting, lowering shades, raising the screen, and dimming the lights.

It was a whole lot fancier than anything they would probably need, but it was good to know that if they ended up lying low for a while, they could do so in comfort.

He stepped down and out of the vehicle in time to wave at Bud as he pulled away. Grayson's and his brother's trucks could stay in this lot. A driver could be hired to take them both home if need be.

Renting this RV was proving to be one of his better ideas. From the outside, it looked important. Anyone who arrived in something like this would draw attention. Good. If someone was looking for Kyra, the last thing they would expect would be to look at a country and western star.

He locked up and headed back inside the hotel. There was a little more activity in the lobby. He scanned the faces. Two couples were eating at separate tables. They were older and, therefore, out of the question. A father with a kid hanging off one arm and a plate in the other joined two younger girls and a woman, presumably his wife, at a table by the window. But it was a young couple with a baby that caught his attention.

Grayson shook it off.

The last thing he needed was to think about marriage and kids when he was about to take on a dangerous mission. Being with Ian earlier had started Grayson wondering if something was wrong with him that he hadn't already considered the timing of starting a family of his own. It hadn't even crossed his mind. Maybe his kid brother was wise beyond his years.

Or maybe meeting Kyra had him realizing there might be someone out there he'd be willing to spend the rest of his life with.

14

"Mind if I look at that to check on news about my father?" Kyra asked Ian, pointing to the iPad.

"Go for it," he said, pushing it toward her. He'd reclaimed a seat by the table and had been studying the hotel and Tower layouts ever since Grayson left to meet up with the RV owner. Checking out the window was too risky, so she'd paced the floors until she was afraid she'd wear a hole in the carpet. She needed to occupy her thoughts rather than allow her imagination to run away with her.

She took the iPad before scrolling through a news page. There was nothing new and, thankfully, her story hadn't reached the public yet. It meant the guy at the condo was keeping his real reason for being there a secret. It was in his best interest to pretend to be a thief rather than a kidnapper or assassin. Thief would be the lesser crime.

Speaking of whom, she needed to call the Dallas police station nearest to the condo and see if she could get information about the man.

"Any news?" Ian asked.

She shook her head.

"My friend Zoya called the police at the condo building. The doorman can describe your brother, Zoya, and myself. We might be in greater danger than we realize if the police are looking for us," she reasoned.

"I could have the family's lawyer dig around for information," Ian said.

"Would that be safe?" she asked.

"We have attorney/client privilege, so he wouldn't be able to divulge anything we tell him," he explained.

"Won't the police have questions for him, though?" she asked, afraid to rock the boat.

"Potentially, yes. But he does have an impressive network and could probably call in a favor or two in order to get information about the man," he said.

Kyra nodded. She had a vague idea of how the political system worked in America but no reason before now to dig into any of the details. "Of course."

One thing she was beginning to realize was that a wealthy and powerful family like the Firebrands would have connections, just as her family did. If anyone could find a way to get information, it would be them. She felt a whole lot better about the meetup having Ian and Grayson on her side. She sure wouldn't want to be on the wrong side of either one of them. They were fair, decent, and honorable people. They seemed to live by some cowboy code that made them stick up for what was right. She had a whole lot of respect for people like the Firebrands. Their father and grandfather, however, were a different story.

Trust was huge in her small circle. It could also mean the difference between life and death. Speaking of which, she scanned the news for any signs Charlie had been captured. The complete lack of information was maddening. A small country like hers was barely a blip on the radar. It worked out nicely most of the time, except that now she wished for global attention.

A few more hours and she would see her cousin, she reminded herself as Ian made a call to his family's attorney. Charlie would be at the meetup along with Marko and Pietro. A question she hadn't considered plagued her thoughts...what next?

Ian ended the call as a knock sounded at the door. It was the signal Ian and Grayson had made up. Three fast knocks followed by three slow ones. Grayson slipped inside the door and nodded toward Ian. He scanned the room and gave a slight nod when their eyes met.

"The RV is loaded and ready. It has everything we could possibly need," he said before going into detail about the sleeping arrangements and the fact they could use it for a quick getaway. "Charlie and the others are welcome to come along with us."

Kyra nodded, praying Charlie would be at the meetup.

"I want to be clear, though, that whoever ends up at the meetup has to ditch their phone if they want to come with us," he said.

"But go where?" she asked, wondering if Grayson had that part figured out yet.

"Good question," he said. "I keep thinking you need to buy more time so your father can build an alliance."

Kyra issued a sharp sigh. "I hope it's that simple. We take a couple of days and stay out of sight while my father works his magic. Then, this whole ordeal is put behind us."

"That seems to be the game right now," Grayson said, then bit down on his bottom lip like he was holding back.

"Is there something that you're not saying?" Kyra asked.

The carpet suddenly got interesting to Grayson.

"Go on. Say it. If you have any hesitation about helping me, I need to know what it is," she said with a little more ire than she'd intended.

"What if you didn't meet up with your security team and cousin?" he asked.

"And do what? Stay here?" she asked. "You have to go back to your lives at some point and my team is trained to..." She started to say *keep me alive* but decided against it considering what had happened.

"Understood," Grayson immediately said. "And I get that you want to be reunited with your family and the people you're most comfortable with."

"But?"

"But we've been doing a great job keeping you under the radar and, honestly, you've..." he flashed eyes at her, "your safety has become important to me. I'm taking this personally now and I'd like to see it through until you're safely reunited with your father."

"I would never ask that of you," she stated. He had no idea what he was signing up for. "First of all, I have no idea how long this will drag on, and secondly, I can't be responsible for you and your brother."

"You're not," Grayson said. But she was. If anything happened to either one of them it would be on her head for the rest of her life.

"I appreciate your willingness to put your life on the line for my safety but I can't allow it." On that point, she was firm.

"What if I don't give you a choice?" he asked.

"Then I have to ask if you've always been this stubborn because in case you hadn't noticed, scary men are after me and..."

"They're no different than the poachers we hunt down on our land," Grayson interjected.

A tiny piece of her—the piece that couldn't stand the thought of never seeing Grayson again after the meetup—wished that was true. She somehow doubted it could be. Even if, together, they had dispatched the guy at the condo. A little voice told her the person behind the attack would send someone more competent next time.

"One of us could get a message to Charlie," Ian piped in. "You wouldn't even have to be at the meetup."

"And waste all this preparation?" She laughed, but no one else did. "Okay, so that wasn't a funny joke but there is some truth to it. You have to admit it. I have no idea how long this coup attempt will last."

"Are you concerned about us not being able to go the distance with you?" Grayson asked with a little bit of fire in his eyes.

"If I'm honest, yes," she admitted.

"Then, the worst that can happen is you lie low for a short while until things cool off. You said yourself this could all be over in a snap if your father is able to get into talks with the right people," Grayson continued, undeterred by her protests.

"What about Charlie?" she asked.

"We'll get a message to him," Grayson said.

Kyra chewed on her bottom lip. It was one thing to take temporary help from a friend of her mother's. It was something entirely different to commit these men to an uncertain future with her, especially when it involved a threat to all of their lives.

She shook her head.

"I'm sorry. I need to see him. He will never believe you. I'm certain he's out of his mind with worry after what happened at the condo. He must know by now, and he'll be sickened by it," she said.

"Is he the one who set up the condo as a safe house?" Grayson asked, his eyebrow arched.

"Not personally. No," she said and then it dawned on her why Grayson would ask. "Those arrangements are made by one of my security team and, no, I don't think anyone did it on purpose. Your original idea of someone hacking into Zoya's cell phone makes the best sense."

All of the hairs on the back of her neck pricked. She dismissed it as an overreaction to an unsettling idea. Was there something to it, though?

GRAYSON TOOK A SEAT. He'd said his piece and it was up to Kyra to take him up on his suggestion or not. He would add one more thing, though, as she considered his proposition. "I realize you haven't known me for long but do I seem like a man who stands behind his word?"

She nodded.

"That's all I'm going to say about it," he said. There was no amount of cajoling that could change a mind once it was made up. He'd learned that lesson the hard way over the years. Or maybe it was just growing up among too many stubborn people with strong personalities that convinced him not to waste his breath. Digging his heels in and making demands only pushed others away. Besides, Kyra was intelligent and strong. She knew her own mind. Only she could determine the best route. All he could do was make the offer.

Now that he had, it was time to move on.

Ian's cell buzzed. He glanced at the screen. "It's Harlen."

"What's the family lawyer doing calling you?" Grayson asked as Ian took the call. He held a finger up, indicating he'd explain in a second.

"Your brother asked him to check into the arrest at the condo," Kyra whispered. "I'm guessing this means he has an update."

"I'm here with Grayson. Mind if I put you on speaker?" Ian asked before locking gazes with Grayson.

Harlen must have agreed because Ian tapped the screen and held the cell phone out so everyone could hear. "Grayson is here." His gaze bounced from his brother to Kyra and back. Her staying quiet went without saying.

"I checked into arrests last night made in Turtle Creek, and none fit the description of the crime you mentioned," Harlen stated.

"How can that be?" Grayson asked as Kyra's jaw nearly fell to the carpet.

"It's as simple as that. I triple checked to make sure my sources were accurate and there were no arrests made at the Turtle Creek address you mentioned," Harlen continued. "There were a few drunk and disorderly conduct arrests made in Deep Ellum, but nothing that resembled the crime you told me about in Turtle Creek."

"I happen to know the police were called to a condo," Grayson stated. "I was standing in the room when it happened."

"Okay-y-y-y," Harlen drew out the word. "And you're one hundred percent certain someone was arrested?"

"No. We fled the scene in case there were others," Grayson said.

"That would be you and Ian?" Harlen asked.

"Let's leave it at me and a friend," Grayson said. "My brother wasn't with me at the time."

"Is there a reason the police would cover up the crime?" Harlen asked.

Grayson blew out a breath as he looked to Kyra, who shrugged. The look on her face was concerning. There were questions. None of which she could ask without giving up her identity and the fact she was in the room.

"It's possible the crime scene had been cleaned up before they arrived," Grayson said. "Wouldn't a report be filed anyway?"

"Dallas is a busy place. If there was no evidence that anything had happened, they might walk away without filing a report. Without knowing the details of what went down, it's difficult to assess the situation. Can you provide any further details?" Harlen asked.

Grayson looked to Kyra, who was shaking her head vigorously.

"Not at this time," Grayson said.

"The police receive prank calls," Harlen stated. "If there was nothing to go on at the scene, they might have chalked the call up to a teenager being stupid."

"Thank you for checking into it," Grayson said.

"Any time," Harlen said. "If you come across more details you want me to chase down, I'm here."

Ian and Grayson thanked the lawyer for his time before ending the call.

"I know what we need to do," Grayson said to Kyra. "We need to find the valet, Lance, and ask him what happened the other night. Police would have interviewed him if they didn't find anything suspicious at the condo. He might know something and be able to provide a missing puzzle piece. He could have a description of the guy at the condo or possibly video footage to see who came to get the guy."

"You took a picture of him," she said.

"It doesn't do any good if the police genuinely believe no crime was committed," he pointed out.

"There's politics involved too," she said. "That complicates everything." She flashed eyes at him. "You said Zoya is fine. That's still true, right?"

"Yes. She's home and secure," he said. "The fact she came home alone would signal you're with me instead of her."

"The guy at the condo is alive." She shivered. "He's out there, probably still looking for me."

"Or he's too hot and got called back to wherever he came from," Grayson said.

"Either way, he's a danger. He can describe you," she said before shaking her head. "They can send better people next time, and they will."

15

L ance worked the evening shift. Kyra did a little digging around on the building and discovered exactly what that meant.

"He works from three p.m. to eleven-thirty. There's half hour crossover in between shift change," she reported to Grayson and Ian.

"His shift started half an hour ago," Grayson said. "By the time we grab food in the RV and head south, he'll be alone."

Kyra gasped as a thought practically smacked her in the face. "What if they've hurt him? To keep him from talking or identifying the jerk who showed up that night?"

"We'll cross that bridge when we come to it," Grayson reasoned, whereas her emotions had kicked in. "My sense is that would be leaving too many casualties behind. It would draw even more attention to the building and what possibly happened that night."

"True," she said. His logic was reasonable. The thought of any innocent person being harmed or killed because of her sent another cold shiver racing down her spine. In her escape, she hadn't necessarily considered the collateral damage this ordeal could create. All the more reason to separate herself out from people who didn't sign up to do this job. Grayson and Ian might be offering to stay the course now but they might end up regretting it later. Where would that leave them? They would feel obligated to see this thing through. Their cowboy code or whatever it was called would never allow them to walk away from a commitment.

She would have to do it for them.

For now, though, she would accept their help and find out if Lance had any information that might help identify the condo man.

"Ready?" Grayson asked as he loaded his pocket with his wallet, phone, and keycard. He picked up the RV keys from the table and wrapped lean fingers around them. His brother followed suit.

"I better change," Kyra said, grabbing the bag of clothing and supplies. She rushed into the bathroom and dressed. She slipped her feet into the boots and put on the white cowgirl hat. Passing by the mirror, she stopped in her tracks. The transformation was truly remarkable. She looked nothing like the princess that had walked into this hotel a few days ago. She, of all people, knew looks could be deceiving. In this case, they nailed the country and western overly partied star.

The reaction she got from the men standing near the door, leaning against opposite walls, was priceless. Eyes wide, both stood tall. The surprise stamped on their faces said they approved of the transformation.

"Now, I'm ready," she said, unable to hide her smile.

"After you, Princess," Grayson said as he opened the door.

The reference felt like the highest compliment she could

be paid. She smiled at him as she walked past and then made sure the brim of her hat was low as she entered the hallway. Ian closed the door behind them and she realized he was holding onto a bag. No doubt, the last of the props needed to sell the idea she was a drunk and obnoxious celebrity.

A family of four with two kids younger than ten years old, by the looks of them, was walking toward the trio from the opposite end of the hallway. Kyra figured she needed to test out her character, so she intentionally swayed her hips from side to side, and slurred her words as the couple neared. The man and woman looked to be in their mid to late thirties, and wholesome. So much so that the mom discreetly covered her little boy's eyes as they walked past.

As much as she didn't want to traumatize anyone, her chest filled with pride that she'd pulled off a character that was so alien to her own personality. She was beginning to believe she might be able to pull off this ruse. It was amazing what a person could do in order to save their own life and the lives of those around them.

Now, the trick was seeing if someone who'd actually set eyes on her before could recognize her. Lance was the ultimate litmus test. She could only pray he was fine and they'd find him smiling and working the valet stand in front of the building.

Inside the RV was impressive. The place was built for luxury. Again, a necessary prop in their deception.

"Help yourself to the fridge if you're hungry," Grayson said as he climbed into the driver's seat.

"Will do," Ian said as he walked to the full-size fridge. "It's impressive what can be ordered and delivered in less than a day's notice."

"Everything is so instant here," Kyra said as Grayson

navigated them out of the parking lot and onto the main road. "It's not like that in my country."

"Believe me, most things are not this easy on a ranch either." Ian's comment made her smile. Maybe they all had more in common than she realized.

"I don't even think we have vehicles like this in my country. Too many mountains," she said.

"Texas is about as flat as they come in many parts. Palo Dora Canyon is a whole different ballgame and we have Hill Country near Austin. But most of the landscape here is straightforward," Ian said.

"I looked Texas up on the iPad earlier. This state is bigger than my entire country," she admitted. "In fact, your ranch is probably equal in size to us."

Ian laughed at the first part of her comment. "You know what they say. Everything is bigger in Texas."

She cocked her head to one side.

"Right," Ian said with a nod. "You're not from around here. You wouldn't have heard the saying."

"I have now," she said with a smile. "From what I've observed, there's a lot of truth to the statement."

They ate in silence during the rest of the ride while each took turns heating food. Kyra went all in with carbs and opted for a spaghetti and meatball dinner, while Ian went for some kind of burrito that came with a side of guacamole and pico de gallo. It looked amazing and smelled even better. She would make plans to have a burrito for her next meal but could only hope it wouldn't be necessary. If all went according to plan, she would be reunited with her security squad and cousin, and they'd be on their way out of the country to the next safe house.

It was agreed that Grayson and Ian would switch places on the drive to the Tower, which was a ten- to fifteen-minute drive in no traffic. Kyra would have one of the spaghetti meals ready and waiting after Grayson had a conversation with Lance.

Grayson pulled the RV under the canopy of the condo building a few minutes after Kyra polished off her last bite. She didn't want to think of the spaghetti as her last meal but knew full well things could go dead wrong in the next few hours.

"Is that your guy?" Ian asked Grayson.

"That's Lance," Grayson responded. It had been a crap shoot to show up like this considering this could have been Lance's night off. Luck smiled on them and Grayson hoped he wasn't using all of it up at the beginning of their search for answers. Instead, he decided to take it as a good omen.

"Okay, bro," Ian said, taking over the driver's seat so they could be ready to go at a moment's notice. "Go do your thing."

"I'm coming with you," Kyra said. "Hope that's okay."

Grayson gave her a once-over. "There's no way in my mind Lance will connect you with the person who showed up here the night before last with Zoya."

"He couldn't stop staring at my best friend," Kyra admitted.

"She was fixed up to look like a princess," he said, "but you didn't need a gown and makeup to be beautiful."

His comment caused her cheeks to turn two shades of pink. He liked the color on her but not the embarrassment it signaled.

"Sorry," he said, "I didn't mean to step out of bounds."

"Don't be," she quickly responded with a smile. "I took it as a compliment."

He nodded and then exited the vehicle, helping her take the couple of steps down from steps that appeared from underneath the vehicle when the door unlocked.

Lance hopped up from the stool next to the door. His gaze snapped to Kyra and fixed for a few seconds before he cleared his throat and made eye contact with Grayson. Lance's eyes widened and he compressed his lips. He seemed surprised that Grayson was back.

"How can I help you, sir?" Lance asked. He had recognized Grayson, so the formal routine was an act. Too late to go back now.

"First of all, I think we both know that I'm not a 'sir' so you don't have to call me that. Remember?" Grayson asked, seeing if he could needle Lance a little bit and throw him off his game.

"I see a lot of people every day. It's impossible to remember everyone. Sorry, s—"

He stopped himself before saying the word again. Good choice. He also shifted his weight from foot to foot and nervously tugged at the ticket in between his fingers.

"We can play that game if you want, but I'd like to know what happened the night before last after I hightailed it out of here," Grayson said, leaning in. "And you can drop the act. You remember me. We both know it." Grayson reached into his pocket and pulled out a hundred-dollar bill. He shook Lance's hand, placing the bill in the guy's palm in the process.

Lance shoved the tip in his front pocket as he glanced around.

"I'm not trying to put you in a bad position here, Lance.

But it's important that I know exactly what happened," Grayson stated.

The valet seemed to be evaluating his options.

"I've been told by management not to talk about it with anyone," Lance finally said. "It could make the building look bad and my manager doesn't want to freak out any of the residents."

"Why would that happen?" Grayson asked. At least he had the young guy talking.

Lance shrugged.

"People freak out over a bug in their condo," Lance said.

"Lance, I need you to tell me exactly what happened," Grayson continued as Kyra stepped behind him.

"Someone must have gotten inside the building without going through the front door," he said. "At first, I thought it might be you, because this all happened not too long after you went bolting out of here with those women."

Grayson made eyes like Lance shouldn't talk about 'those women' in front of the one standing behind him.

It seemed to dawn on Lance how uncomfortable that might be for her. He gave a slight nod before continuing. "So, I'm here doing my job when a pair of dudes walk past me into the front door. I told them to stop but one opens his jacket and I see metal. He stops and then walks over to me, telling me that I never saw them. He asks me if I understand and I tell him that I do."

"Can you describe the men?" Grayson asked.

"One was tall and bald. He had some kind of accent I've ever heard before," Lance admits. "I didn't get a good look at the other guy. He keeps his face in the opposite direction of me the whole time. He's a few inches shorter than Baldy but all chest. He looks like he's about to bust out of his suit. He has black hair and it's slicked back into a ponytail.

That's all I know about him. They tell me that I need to keep my eyes on the concrete because they're going to come back. They tell me that if I see what happens next, they have to kill me."

"What did you do?" Grayson asked.

"Exactly what they said. I kept my eyes to the ground and they let me live," he stated. "Not ten minutes pass when a squad car comes squealing up to the front door. There were two cops inside and they both tell me to watch their vehicle as they bolted inside the building."

"I'm guessing they didn't find anyone," Grayson said. Kyra slipped her hand inside his and gave a slight squeeze. He tugged her closer to him and she hugged his arm using his body as a shield.

"Not to my knowledge," Lance explained. He threw his hands up in the air. "They asked if I'd seen anyone."

Grayson took in a breath and readied himself to be told that Lance gave him up to the cops. "And what did you say?"

"I told them it had been quiet all evening," Lance said. "They asked about building security and I told them the camera was broken, which was true."

"So there's no footage to prove any of this?" Grayson asked.

"Afraid not," Lance said. "The strangest thing is that the cameras were working up until fifteen minutes before you arrived."

"You don't say," Grayson didn't bother to hide his shock.

"I wondered if you had something to do with it," Lance said.

"Me? No," Grayson reassured. "I came to pick up my friends and got surprised by one of their exes."

Lance nodded, but his face pinched as he seemed to be trying to connect dots that didn't quite connect. It was like working a math problem backward and realizing the numbers didn't add up.

"Did anyone else show up?" Grayson wondered if Charlie or any of the rest of her security team had made it to the first safe house.

"It was a crazy night," Lance admitted. "Anything's possible."

Grayson nodded. With no security camera footage, it would be impossible to tell if Kyra's security team showed.

"I appreciate you not mentioning me to the police," Grayson said.

"You seemed like a nice guy and like you were trying to help those women." Lance's face morphed into an apology after bringing them up again.

"Thanks for the information," Grayson said. He realized there were holes in building security and the cameras could easily have been taken down remotely. This safe house wasn't exactly safe. "You've been a huge help."

"Ask him how old the men were," Kyra whispered before squeezing his hand.

"Late thirties or something like that." Lance shrugged. "I'm not great with guessing ages."

He turned in time to see Kyra's face turn bleached-sheet white.

"My cousin," she mouthed.

Grayson craned his neck around to see Lance again. "Any chance you saw a guy with light red hair?"

"No. No one like that," Lance stated.

"I have to get word to my father. There's no gang behind this like we were led to believe," she whispered. "It's an inside job."

As Grayson turned toward the RV, the crack of a bullet split the air.

16

"Go inside, lock the doors, and call 911," Grayson shouted to Lance. When the young guy didn't move, Grayson shouted, "Go!"

Kyra bolted toward the opened RV door, tugging Grayson by the hand along with her. The next few minutes ticked by in slow motion. Lance made it inside the building in time for another shot to be fired. A bullet shattered the glass. Lance took a step back before the color red flowered on the left shoulder of his white polo shirt. But his expression would be etched in Kyra's mind for the rest of her life.

Grayson spun around. "Get inside the vehicle with my brother."

Kyra couldn't leave Lance to die. She mumbled an apology before shooting toward the glass doors that were now open. Grayson was a step behind her, probably using his body to shield her. He would have turned around and run into the building to help Lance anyway.

Much to her surprise, Ian was a few steps behind them with his cell phone to his ear. He'd locked up the RV and was on their heels, ushering everyone inside.

Marko came bolting through the lobby from behind, a look of concern on his face. Was it possible he wasn't involved? Had Pietro gone off the rails? And where was Charlie? Ten minutes away trying to meet up with her at the Tower?

Her heart couldn't accept the fact her cousin could be involved. There was no way in her mind it was a possibility.

"Freeze right there," Grayson said to Marko, stepping in between him and Kyra.

"Do you know who I am?" Marko asked. "Tell them, Kyra."

"Why, Marko? Why would you do it? Money? Greed? My father brought you into the family and gave you a job. And this is how you repay him?" Kyra slipped her hand in the back pocket of her jeans shorts where she'd hid a metal case as Pietro came running in from the glass doors.

"Thank heaven you're safe, Princess," Pietro said, chest heaving.

"Do either of you believe I'm that naïve? Do you not realize I see what's happening here?" Kyra couldn't hold back her emotions. "Where's Charlie?"

Pietro looked at Marko as Ian tended to Lance.

"I'm sorry, Princess," was all Pietro said before he reached behind his back presumably to retrieve a weapon.

Kyra wasted no time spinning around and throwing a star that landed right between Pietro's eyes. All the hurt and betrayal welling up inside her like a violent storm. It was unimaginable to think the people she'd trusted could turn on her, on her father, and on their country. And for what? Money? Power? Greed. Marko dove toward her, tackling her at the waist, knocking her off balance. The next thing she knew the crack of a bullet split the air. She gasped as she said a quick protection prayer. She kicked Marko, landing a foot to the groin as he grabbed fistfuls of her clothing. In the next second, he was reaching behind her as she struggled to stay on her feet. Twisting and turning, she tried to break free from his grip. But he was strong. Too strong.

No matter how much she kicked, punched, and screamed, he overpowered her, wrestling her to the ground.

The next thing she knew, Marko was being picked up and tossed off her. Grayson fired off a kick. Marko grunted but then spun around and swept Grayson's knees, knocking him off balance.

Kyra could only watch as the two men fought.

"You, bitch," Pietro said from behind her as he fired off another shot. She moved out of the way in time for the bullet to whiz past her ear. By the time she spun around to face him, Ian was on top of him, straddling him, firing off punch after punch as blood squirted from Pietro's nose and mouth.

Ian wrestled the gun out of Pietro's hand before firing off a punch that knocked the man out cold. Ian slipped off his belt and tied Pietro's hands behind his back for when he came to. By the time she turned to Marko, Grayson had done a number on her now-former security guard.

Lance was bleeding, so Kyra ran over to him. She helped him off with his shirt as the welcomed sound of sirens filled the evening sky.

"My cousin..." she said to Grayson.

"Go," Ian said. "I'll take care of the situation here. Come back for me when you find Charlie."

"Are you sure?" Grayson asked.

Ian shooed them away. Before they left, Grayson gave his brother a bear hug that melted the rest of Kyra's resolves.

Inside the RV, she took the passenger seat as Grayson claimed the driver's side.

"You were amazing back there," he said as he hit the gas pedal to the floor.

"So were you," she said. "I just hope Lance will be all right."

"From what I saw, he took a hit to the shoulder," Grayson said. "There's a lot of blood, but he's young and seems otherwise healthy. I think he'll make it."

Kyra blew out the breath she'd been holding. "I owe you and Ian my life."

"You handled yourself pretty damn well back there," he said. "We just gave the assist."

"I have to get word to my father," she said. "But first, I need to find Charlie."

Grayson rolled up in front of the Hyatt so fast he practically peeled rubber. He exited the RV and shouted something at the valet, who nodded. Then, he linked their fingers as they bolted through the expansive lobby and toward the Tower.

At the coffee shop, a redhead caught her eye. She squeezed Grayson's hand to stop him from running. Tears filled her eyes as she recognized her cousin's face. His head was down and he looked frightened out of his mind, but he was here. Safe.

Kyra walked right up to him. He glanced up and almost dismissed her. But then he locked gazes with her. And then she knew he recognized her. She ran the couple of steps toward him and wrapped her cousin in a hug.

"Charlie, it's me. Kyra," she said as relief flooded her. She fought back the torrent of tears threatening, reminding herself that he was here. He was alive and standing right in front of her.

"Kyra?" There was a mix of shock and relief in his tone. "It's you?"

"It's me, Charlie," she reassured. "I'm here."

Charlie hugged her even tighter. "I don't know what I would have done if anything had happened to you." Charlie's voice shook and she realized how difficult it was for him to contain his emotions. "You're the only little sister I have."

White, hot tears streamed down Kyra's face, a mix of relief and hope that not everything was lost. "I'm here. I'm okay. I'm not going anywhere."

Charlie pulled back and examined her, like he needed visual reassurance of the facts. "You really are alive."

She nodded and smiled. "I am. However, we need to get word to my father about Marko and Pietro. They're back at the condo and should already be in the back of a police vehicle."

"We figured out who was behind this when they blackmailed me. I overheard Marko plotting against your father and then had to pretend not to know what he and Pietro were planning as we 'looked' for you. They were planning to keep me alive because you trust me. Your father couldn't say anything publicly until you were found safe," Charlie said. He pulled out his cell and fired off a text. "Now, he knows you're alive and well. Interpol will take care of the arrests on our end." After explaining, Charlie's gaze shifted behind her to the man standing a few steps behind, waiting, patient. "Who is he and why is he here?"

"This is Grayson Firebrand," Kyra said, taking a couple of steps back and reaching for his hand.

"Firebrand?" Charlie said, looking like a whole lot of dots were connecting. "As in your mother's friend from America?"

"It's good to meet you," Grayson said to Charlie. "And the answer to your question is *yes*. Our mothers were friends."

"It's really good to meet you," Charlie said with a warm smile. Then, bouncing topics, he turned to Kyra and asked, "How did you find out about Marko and Pietro?"

"Long story," she said. "And one I plan to tell you over a hot meal and a cold beer."

Charlie exhaled, and his shoulders deflated. It was like he'd barely been holding it together until he found her again. He brought Kyra into another hug. "I still can barely believe you're standing here in front of me."

Kyra glanced around after the embrace. "We should probably get out of a public area until we receive confirmation everyone involved has been arrested."

"Right," Charlie said, looking a little lost as to their next move.

"I have an RV waiting at the hotel," Grayson said. "I think you'll find it comfortable enough."

Charlie nodded, more of those tears streaming down his cheeks. He tapped his cell phone a few times before holding it up. "Your dad knows you're safe now."

Kyra couldn't wait to see her father again but she realized palace life wasn't for her. She would find a way to tell her father she wanted, no needed, freedom instead. Now was not the time. Now, they needed to pick up Ian and celebrate.

Grayson held her hand on the way to the RV. Charlie raised an eyebrow at the move but didn't ask questions. He settled into the RV as Kyra pulled out a few cold beers. She handed one over to her cousin as they made the drive to pick up Ian at Turtle Creek.

"Where do we go from here?" she asked after giving their statements to the police.

"We should stay out of sight for a day or two." Grayson checked his cell phone. "There's an RV park not too far from here. We could stop there for the night and regroup."

"Will there be people around?" Charlie asked.

"Probably not too many," Grayson reassured.

"That sounds nice," Kyra said.

"I'll go anywhere as long as we get to stay in this vehicle," Charlie said, some of his stress seemed to be peeling off as he took a drink of the cold brew.

True to his word, the park was close, the drive short. The spot Grayson secured had a lake view that was beautiful. Kyra excused herself to the bedroom and then changed into a jogging outfit as they settled in.

When she returned to the main living area, Grayson looked into her eyes, took her by the hand, and asked, "Take a walk with me?"

Her heart skipped a few beats and her stomach free fell as she nodded. "I'd like that a lot actually."

GRAYSON LINKED his and Kyra's fingers as they walked to the water's edge. The moon was full and chirps of cicadas filled the night air. It was almost musical and made him miss home. Except he realized home wouldn't be the same after meeting this incredible woman. And he needed to take a shot at telling her his feelings.

"Kyra, I've never met anyone like you before. And I suspect that I never will again either," Grayson began. "You can turn around and walk out of my life forever, but not without knowing how I feel about you first."

He took a knee in front of her. She gasped, bringing a hand up to cover her mouth as he took the other one in his.

"In some ways, we barely know each other," he continued. "For example, I don't know your favorite flower or whether or not you drink sweet tea or plain."

The last part drew her eyebrows together in question. The fact she didn't realize sweet tea or plain was a major question in the south and southwest made him smile.

"But I don't need to know those insignificant details because I know you're brave and sincere. You have a wicked sense of humor and the kindest heart I believe I've ever seen. And I'm the last guy I ever thought would be saying what I'm about to say, but I've fallen in love with you, fast and hard." He risked looking up and locked onto her gaze. He could see tears welling in her eyes and had no idea if they were a good sign or not. At this point, he didn't care. Couldn't care. Because he knew one thing was certain. If he didn't tell her how he felt right now, he would regret it for the rest of his life.

Spill out his feelings and put his heart on the line now and he could accept the outcome. Even if she didn't love him back, at least he'd tried. He'd given it all he had. She'd be crystal clear on his feelings, leaving no room for doubt.

If she didn't love him back, well, that was drawing a bad hand. The spark in her eyes every time they locked gazes made him believe different. It made him think there was a chance at the two of them making a go in life together.

Kyra didn't immediately speak.

"I know this is a lot to throw at you, but you should know that I would love the chance to spend the rest of our days with me learning every little thing and big thing about you. How you take your coffee. Whether or not you put syrup on your pancakes or like a little bowl to the side to dip each bite in. I want to spend the rest of my life learning your favorite flower and if you like dark or milk chocolate," he said. "As wild as this all may sound, I believe in my heart of hearts that we could make a run at forever. That I'd like to make a go at 'the rest of our lives' spent memorizing each other's habits and quirks."

She stood there, speechless as a tear leaked from one of her eyes. He took it as a bad sign but pressed on anyway. Because when a man finds the rare woman he sees his entire future with, he keeps going until she tells him to stop.

"And I want to hold our children in my arms and, as out in left field as this might be, have family surrounding us. I do realize how impossible this all might be logistically and you might not want any of these things least of all with me," he continued. "But if you're willing to take the leap with me, I promise to love you until my last breath here on this earth and find you in eternity if only to hold you in my arms again."

Grayson exhaled the breath he'd been holding. There wasn't much more he could say than what he just did. He'd explained his feelings, told her how he saw their now and their future unfolding. It might be too much for her. She might turn away from him and never look back. But at least she knew. She could make the decision whether or not to grab hold of him or run in the opposite direction but the facts were out there, his heart was on his sleeve, and she had the power to crush him with a few words.

"Are you serious about everything you said just now?" she asked, and he realized for the first time in the conversation that she seemed a little taken back by his confession.

"One hundred percent," he said. "But if it's too much to grasp all at once, we can take it slow. I just want to be in your life."

"I have another question," she said, scraping her teeth across her bottom lip.

He nodded, preparing for the worst.

"Are you asking me to marry you?" She brought her other hand up to her mouth, clasping the two together.

"Yes, Kyra, I'm asking you if you would do me the incredible honor of marrying me?" he asked. Might as well go all in with the question that was the one he wanted to ask anyway. His heart pounded his ribcage as he waited for any hint as to which way this conversation might turn.

"Kyra Firebrand," she said with a smile that sent warmth rocketing through him. She nodded. "It's a beautiful name...yes?"

"I can't think of a better one," he said as she practically beamed at him. He took her hand in his and could feel hers trembling. "Will you marry me?"

"Yes, Grayson. I'll marry you. And I want all those things you said. Plenty of children and family around but most of all I want to spend the rest of my life with you. I've fallen in love with you and can't imagine building a life with anyone else," she said. "And it's a good thing you asked me to marry you or I would have had to have been the one to ask."

Grayson stood and hauled his fiancée against his chest and then looped his arms around her waist. She fit him perfectly as he dipped his head down and claimed those gorgeous lips of hers. She parted her lips and teased his tongue inside her mouth.

He pulled back first and locked gazes with her. He could look into those beautiful eyes all day.

"I have questions, though," she said.

"Shoot," he said.

"Where will we live?" she asked. "I can't leave my father alone in his condition."

"Do you have to live in your country all the time?" he asked.

"I guess not, but how would that work exactly?" Concern lines wrinkled her forehead.

"I'm needed the most at the ranch during calving season. I'm figuring we can split the difference. Live on the ranch half of the year and in your country for the rest of the time. I've been watching my brother Brax go on tour with Raleigh and they're making it work. There's no reason we can't do the same thing," he surmised. The truth was that he'd do anything to ensure the two of them were together, even if it meant moving overseas full-time.

Because when it came to Kyra, one word came to mind...*home*. Kyra was the home he never knew he needed or wanted, for that matter. Nothing had been missing in his life until he met her. Losing her would create a lifelong ache.

But she'd said yes, and they were going to spend the rest of their lives getting to know each other. His Kyra. His bride. His princess.

His home no matter where they hung their hats at night.

"Yes to all of that," Kyra said.

Grayson dipped his head down and kissed his soon-to-be bride.

A royal wedding? Ian didn't even know where to start with that one. All he knew for certain was that he needed to get a whole lot closer to the only other single brother he had left. Hudson.

Hudson was as likely to get married as Ian. The two needed to start their own club or he was going to have to make friends with the other side of the family. At twenty-eight years-old, he had plenty of time to find someone. Hudson was only a year older. Technically, almost two, but who was counting?

Neither seemed in a rush.

Besides, there'd only been one person who'd caused the kinds of feelings in Ian that might make him consider throwing on a tuxedo...Daphne Thompson. Since he hadn't seen her since high school graduation and she was most likely married with kids by now, there was no chance he'd be putting a ring on her finger.

He knew he'd had it bad for someone when he still thought about her and no one could measure up ten years later.

Ian sat on the porch of the main house, thinking how quickly life could change. Seven of his brothers were married or planning a wedding. If God himself had come down from the heavens at the beginning of this past summer and told Ian seven of his brothers would be off the dating market by fall, he wouldn't have been convinced.

Lucky for him, his only temptation was nowhere to be seen. He'd lost track of her years ago, on purpose. When she'd laughed at his proposal at eighteen before taking off to Austin, he'd untangled himself from everyone and everything that could remind him of their relationship. She was probably right to break it off. What were the odds of a high school relationship making it for the long haul? During his heartbreak summer that had followed the breakup, he'd been told only two percent of high school relationships ended up in marriage. Of the ones who did marry, only half survived to the ten-year-anniversary mark.

So, yeah, the odds had been stacked against them from the first time he'd held her hand and realized she was special.

The front door opened and Grayson stepped outside.

"Shouldn't you be in there planning your wedding?" Ian asked his brother. Grayson and Kyra were going to make a great couple. His brother had never been happier and Ian was genuinely happy for him. The same ridiculous smile that seemed plastered on most of his brothers' faces recently upturned the corners of Grayson's mouth. He had that same lovestruck look in his eyes at the mention of Kyra.

"Turns out, when you marry royalty, there are a whole bunch of planners who do the heavy lifting," Grayson said, then motioned to the rocker next to Ian. "Mind if I sit?"

"Not at all." Ian took a closer look at his brother and realized something else was going on. His mind snapped to their father, who was still recovering from a recent stroke. "Everything all right?"

"With me? Never better," Grayson said. He leaned forward, clasping his hands and resting his elbows on his knees. This didn't signal good news.

"What is it?" Ian asked. "What's going on?"

"Can't a brother just sit here for a while?" Grayson asked, but there was something bothering him.

"Not with that look on his face," Ian retorted. "Is the family okay?"

Grayson nodded.

"Something up with Kyra?" Ian pressed.

"No. Nothing like that," Grayson said before compressing his lips into a frown.

"Then, what?" Ian asked in a little more demanding tone this time.

"This news has to do with you," Grayson said.

"Me?" Ian really was confused now. He made a show of checking over his body. "I'm a little bruised up from the fight in Dallas but there's nothing wrong with—"

"She's coming back," Grayson said, studying his hands. A few seconds ticked by before his brother turned to look at him. "Daphne is moving back to Lone Star Pass."

"And that's my business because?" Those words came out a little more heated than Ian had intended. The irony that he'd been sitting here thinking about her a few seconds ago wasn't lost on him.

"I hear she's in bad shape," Grayson said. "She's had a rough go in Austin and we—"

"Hold on right there. Whose *we*?" Ian asked, well aware he'd just interrupted his brother. It wasn't like Ian to be rude. The news rattled him more than he cared to admit.

"The family," Grayson clarified.

"So...what? You guys just had a meeting about me or something? Is that it?" Ian's defenses were on high alert. Even though he realized what was happening, he was having trouble reining it in.

"You know it wasn't," Grayson said calmly. He stood up. "I'll leave you alone to process. We just wanted to be the ones to tell you first."

With that, his brother turned and then walked back inside the house.

Ian wasn't real sure what to think about this news. Daphne could live anywhere she pleased. Lone Star Pass was her home too. Her return would have no effect on his life...right?

CLICK here to keep reading Ian and Daphne's story.

ALSO BY BARB HAN

Texas Firebrand

Rancher to the Rescue

Disarming the Rancher

Rancher under Fire

Rancher on the Line

Undercover with the Rancher

Rancher in Danger

Set-up with the Rancher

Rancher under the Gun

Taking Cover with the Rancher

Don't Mess With Texas Cowboys

Texas Cowboy's Protection

Texas Cowboy Justice

Texas Cowboy's Honor

Texas Cowboy Daddy

Texas Cowboy's Baby

Texas Cowboy's Bride

Texas Cowboy's Family

Cowboys of Cattle Cove

Cowboy Reckoning

Cowboy Cover-up

Cowboy Retribution

For more of Barb's books, visit www.BarbHan.com.

ABOUT THE AUTHOR

Barb Han is a USA TODAY and Publisher's Weekly Best-selling Author. Reviewers have called her books "heartfelt" and "exciting."

Barb lives in Texas—her true north—with her adventurous family, a poodle mix and a spunky rescue who is often referred to as a hot mess. She is the proud owner of too many books (if there is such a thing). When not writing, she can be found exploring Manhattan, on a mountain either hiking or skiing depending on the season, or swimming in her own backyard.

Sign up for Barb's newsletter at www.BarbHan.com.

Printed in Great Britain
by Amazon